In the Pursuit of Catherine

Jae Maxson

iUniverse, Inc.
New York Bloomington

In the Pursuit of Catherine

iUniverse books may be ordered through booksellers or by contacting:

iUniverse
1663 Liberty Drive
Bloomington, IN 47403
www.iuniverse.com
1-800-Authors (1-800-288-4677)

Because of the dynamic nature of the Internet, any Web addresses or links contained in this book may have changed since publication and may no longer be valid. The views expressed in this work are solely those of the author and do not necessarily reflect the views of the publisher, and the publisher hereby disclaims any responsibility for them.

ISBN: 978-1-4502-1778-1 (sc)
ISBN: 978-1-4502-1780-4 (dj)
ISBN: 978-1-4502-1779-8 (e-book)

Printed in the United States of America

iUniverse rev. date:3/23/2010

Prologue

Adam knew the routine: place the order, sign the bill, pull the truck around, and help the dock men with the loading. Most other customers didn't help. They were content to stay in their trucks, smoking cigarettes or listening to the radio. Adam was different. His work ethics ran deep.

The mud squished between the tread of his boots as he jumped from the driver's seat and walked alongside his flatbed. Every pick up was the same. The lot attendant was always talkative and full of questions. The forklift driver was disgruntled and hurried. The attendant met Adam at the loading dock, smiling widely from beneath his yellow hardhat.

"This one must be yours," the attendant stated as the forklift sputtered toward them, laden with an eight foot pickup truck bed swaying from its chains. Its pace slowed as the machine inched toward the awaiting flatbed. The attendant and Adam each held onto opposite sides of the box, guiding it carefully so as not to damage its metallic shine.

Within a second, all of that was forgotten-- a distant dream. The forklift was silent. Adam's hands had gone numb, and the attendant worked for each breath. The forklift driver had gone for help, leaving the two men alone.

Adam remembered it like the start of a race, but instead the firing of a gun that sends eager runners over the starting line, the sound was the distinct snapping of the forklift chain. It was an unfamiliar sound, having never been heard before that day. It was a sound followed by a sequence of desperate and horrific acts.

Adam didn't register his pain at first. He rushed over to the attendant, unaware of the blood that streamed down his own face and speckled his white shirt.

"It's going to be all right."

"I can't breathe. You've got to help me," the attendant begged, straining for air. He reached to grasp Adam's hand for some kind of strength. "You've got to get this thing off of me."

"Help's on the way, buddy. Just hang on."

"I can't wait! I can't breathe!" His voice was punctuated by a cough that spewed scarlet blood.

Feeling that he had no choice, Adam stood to full height and gulped in a huge dose of oxygen. With a prayer for superhuman strength, he lifted up with all his might.

"Okay," he huffed. "Roll out from beneath. Hurry! I can't hold it very long." His entire frame began to shake from the weight of the treacherous box, and he felt his fingers begin to slip. The box then fell, like a gavel on the life of the young man. Silence hung suspended in the air where the box should still be hanging.

Kneeling once again beside the now silent attendant, Adam stared at what he had done, waiting to wake up. But the ending of this dream never came. Even when help arrived to lift the box off its victim, he was still dreaming. The only feeling was the chill of the needle that swam back and forth, closing the wound to his forehead.

"Can you describe what happened?"

Adam looked up at the uniformed man who seemed to have materialized out of nowhere. Adam glanced down at his blood-saturated shirt, as if realizing for the first time that he had been hurt as well. When he looked back up at the officer, his eyes were glazed and gripped with hurt.

"Sir, are you going to be all right?"

"Yes. I…" he stopped and focused on the lifeless body lying yards away. "Why couldn't it have been me?"

Chapter One

To anyone else, a single-engine plane ride above a seemingly endless swamp would have been boring. To Catherine Scott it was exhilarating. As a journalist for a small town newspaper, she had covered her share of country stories-- but never before had she been airborne for an interview.

Mr. Colton, the owner of the small airplane, had insisted that she join him for the routine pesticide spraying. He had claimed that she would not be able to accurately inform the public of the process without experiencing it first-hand.

Now she sat surveying the swampy countryside while Mr. Colton explained the mechanics of spraying. Catherine wasn't the least bit interested in the subject but still took in every word. She loved to write her articles in such a way that even the dullest of stories would catch the reader's wandering attention.

After landing and parking the airplane, Mr. Colton answered the last of the questions on Catherine's list. She took down the remainder of the interview with a few more scribbled lines and made her way to her car. After taking a seat behind the wheel, she took a moment to straighten her wind-blown hair, thankful for the shelter afforded by her somewhat secure car from the breezy October day.

Turning the key, she said a quick prayer of thanks as her car once again proved its immortality. Catherine had every intention of running this car into the ground. Only then would she buy a more reliable one. The last thing she would ever want was for some overworked mechanic to fix the many problems, only to tell her that she owed hundreds of dollars beyond his estimated quote.

The possibility of being stranded in a snowstorm with a car that refused to operate was always in the back of her mind, but she was determined to cross that bridge when she got to it. For now she just began her journey back to the office. She had an article to write.

Catherine found her best friend and coworker Megan Walker right where she'd left her; eyes glued to the computer screen, pretending to write an article while actually surfing the internet.

"How's your story coming, Meg?"

Slowly turning from the computer, Megan did nothing to hide the fact that she had been slacking. "This one's going to make me famous. No matter how fast I type, my fingers never seem to keep up with my mind. You know how it is."

"Unfortunately, no I don't," Catherine answered as she took a seat at her own desk, which was adjacent to her friend. "I actually have to think about the words before I write them." She shook her head. "In all these years we've been roommates, I have yet to figure out how you do so little and still get paid for it."

"There are some things you just can't learn at college. So, how'd the interview go?" Megan questioned.

"Surprisingly well. The pilot insisted that I take a ride in the crop-duster."

"I thought you were doing a story about pesticide sprayers."

"They're one and the same."

Megan nodded and then went back to her typing. Catherine followed suit and began an outline for her story.

Only fifteen minutes passed before they were interrupted by the sound of feet scuffing on the floor behind them. Catherine stole a glance at Megan who dramatically rolled her eyes.

"Time for the three o'clock, girls," Mr. Cady announced as he shuffled toward the conference room.

Catherine picked up her notebook and pen and rose to follow her boss into the second of two daily meetings. Glancing down, she silently shook her head at how his feet never quite lifted off the floor. It was as if he were too lazy or tired to take complete steps; so instead, he just pushed his feet along to his intended destination. His unkempt appearance, along with the permeating odor of cough drops and aftershave, made him the most unlikely editor of the most widely circulated newspaper in the county. But, under his distasteful exterior was a smart man who, despite a serious lack of communication skills, had sustained a very successful business for more than twenty years.

Once inside the conference room, Mr. Cady walked to the front of the room and took a seat at the head of the table. Any other boss might have stood, causing the occupants of the room to look up at him, but not Mr. Cady.

"I trust everyone's day has been productive," he began as the employees opened their various folders to report the status of their assigned stories. Catherine did the same, just as she had done for the last four years. The meeting carried on in the usual fashion until Mr. Cady rose and addressed the occupants of the room in his own special manner.

"This coming week will be my last as editor."

Astonished, Catherine looked from Mr. Cady to Megan, who had stopped doodling on her notebook and looked up to meet her friend's gaze. Catherine just shrugged, indicating that she had no idea what the boss was talking about.

"I have decided to retire. For the last three months I have been searching for my replacement. Your new editor will be working with me for a week while I show him the way things operate. After that,

3

he will be in charge. I thank you all for your hard work, and I ask that you will show the new editor the same respect you have never failed to show me. Things will be different around here. Whether you're apprehensive or ready for the change, I know you won't be disappointed."

He silently reached to sort the papers scattered on the table in front of him. His audience was speechless as they watched. When he had secured his overstuffed folder beneath his arm, he smiled down at his faithful employees.

"Have a safe weekend everyone," he said softly before exiting the room. All eyes remained fixed for a few moments on the door through which he had just passed.

Catherine could feel Megan's eyes on her and knew she was dying to talk about the last half hour's turn of events, but it would have to wait. They would have plenty of time to discuss it when they got home.

Two hours later the women sat at their small kitchen table, sipping fresh cider and discussing Mr. Cady's unexpected retirement.

"Personally, I'm glad to see the old coot leave," Megan admitted.

"I know that he's not the most congenial man, but he's always been good to work for. He's always taken care of his employees and treated them fairly."

"Oh stop sticking up for him. You know just as well as I that Mr. Cady is a boring, lifeless man who, while we're on the subject, gives me the creeps."

Catherine smiled at her friend's never ending bluntness.

"I'm not going to argue that he has his own unique personality, Meg, but I know that I could have had a worse boss for the last four years," she said cautiously. Megan was her best friend and they shared close to everything, but the one thing they did not share was the same faith. It had never caused her to question Megan's friendship, but she knew that she was under constant scrutiny. Every sentence and action was carefully thought out, hopefully reducing the risk of having her own beliefs thrown back in her face.

"I'm just anxious about Monday. Mr. Cady said we wouldn't be disappointed, but I'm more than a little skeptical," Catherine said. "I wonder what the new editor is like."

"Tall, dark and handsome of course."

Both women shared a laugh at the thought, and Megan went on to complain about not having a date for tonight. Catherine listened in silent amusement, trying to remember the last time she'd even been on a date.

The girls' Friday evening turned into a late night of movies and popcorn. When Catherine's head hit her pillow, she was too tired to think over the day's events. It was just as well with her. She knew that worrying over it wouldn't change the fact that things were going to be different in the weeks to come. How different, she didn't know. Nor did she know if the change would be for better or for worse. Either way, Monday was already coming and there was no stopping it.

Catherine was relieved to find the office bustling with its normal activity at eight o'clock Monday morning. Nothing seemed out of the ordinary. The line to the coffee maker was just as long as usual. The same handful of employees who had a tendency to be late each day was just beginning to trickle in. The only difference was the anxiety in the air.

It seemed like forever for nine o'clock to roll around, but it eventually surfaced, bringing the morning meeting with it. Catherine walked slowly into the conference room with all of the other personnel, anticipating the introduction of their new boss. The group nonchalantly filed in, pretending not to notice the stranger standing at the head of the table. When every seat had been taken, the man addressed the group.

"Good morning, everyone. I'm Lyndon Reinhardt. From now on I'll be acting as your editor."

Catherine looked from her new employer to Mr. Cady, who had humbly taken a seat toward the corner of the room. She noted the incredible difference in appearance between the two men. Mr. Cady sat with back slouched, speaking volumes about his demeanor. His hair was ruffled and his tie was half-hidden beneath a checkered sweater vest that had lost its glory decades ago.

Turning her inspection back to Mr. Reinhardt, she couldn't find a wrinkle on his suit. His face was cleanly shaven, and his dark hair was trimmed so perfectly that Catherine wondered if he was married to a cosmetologist. A very distinct jaw line gave him a look of authority that, she assumed, he often used to his advantage.

"Earlier, I was observing your morning rituals." He stopped and took a very slow look around the room making eye contact with each individual. When he came to Catherine, she found herself thinking over the last hour wondering if he had seen her do anything distasteful. Her mind came up blank so she focused her attention back to the front of the room.

"Five of you were late. That will not be tolerated. I remind you that our workday begins at eight. Perhaps you have decided that since the morning meeting doesn't begin until nine, you can show up whenever you feel like it. From now on the meeting will begin at eight-thirty. That means your coffee will be finished, and you will be in your seats at eight-thirty."

Not one objection was voiced. In fact, the room was completely silent-- but Catherine could see the dread on every face. Even Mr. Cady looked a little scared, like he wondered if he had made a mistake in hiring the demanding Mr. Reinhardt. Catherine could sympathize with him. She felt like a grade-schooler being scolded by an aged teacher with a ruler in his hand.

"I observed at least three people out of dress code. Yes, there is a dress code, in case you've forgotten. Men, this is not a football game, and ladies, this is not a cocktail party. Lastly, personal cell phones are for personal use. That means they are to be used on personal time. Texting your boyfriend or girlfriend is not company business. Therefore, it should not be conducted on company time."

"Well, now that we've been introduced, let's get on with the morning assignments."

Past that point the meeting showed signs of normality. Mr. Reinhardt seemed strict, but from what Catherine could gather in the remaining fifteen minutes of the meeting, he was indeed qualified for the job.

When the meeting broke up, Catherine headed straight for her desk. Megan wasn't far behind her and purposefully cleared her throat to get her friend's attention. She looked up just long enough to read her lips. There was no doubt about it; she knew with whom she was sharing lunch today.

"He is so haughty!" Megan declared as soon as she entered the break room. "The way he addressed us made me think I was in the Army."

"He does have a rather demanding look to him," Catherine agreed.

"Oh, his look is the *only* thing I find favorable."

"What do you mean by that?"

"Were you sleeping during the nine o'clock?" Megan asked. "He's gorgeous! With that clean-cut look, definite jaw line, and dark eyes he is totally my type. If it weren't for his detestable personality, that is."

Catherine laughed at her friend's serious conclusion. Megan was always on the hunt for *Mr. Right*. Every man who came within her view was evaluated, picked apart, and scrutinized until she had determined whether or not he would make a suitable companion to grow old with. The duration of the entire process was only a fraction of a second, but she had it down to an art.

On the other hand, while Catherine possessed the human capability to judge physical attraction, she chose to see every man for who he was, not for what he could be. Her main reasoning behind this practice was that it was, first and foremost, biblical. Secondly, she looked beyond initial attraction, or repulsion, because she wished the same to be done to her.

"So, what did you honestly think of him?" Megan persisted.

"It doesn't matter what I think of him, Meg. What matters now is that he's our boss. Mr. Cady wouldn't have chosen him if he hadn't been qualified."

"So, you weren't sleeping during the meeting?"

Catherine thought back to her first glimpse of Mr. Reinhardt. There was no denying that he was the best looking man she'd seen in a long time.

"No. I certainly was not," she answered with a smile.

Chapter Two

The longest Monday Catherine had ever had was finally over. She gathered up her purse and jacket and briskly walked toward the stairs. The moment she set foot on the first step, she remembered that she had forgotten her notebook. Turning quickly on the step, she collided head-on with Mr. Reinhardt's crisp white shirt and tie.

Caught off guard, she stared at her hands where they had landed on his chest. Too embarrassed to look him in the eye, she quickly withdrew her hands and struggled to apologize.

"I'm so sorry," she began and took a step backward, only to realize that there was nothing to step back onto. Her arms flailed through the air, searching for something to save her from falling down the entire flight of stairs. She closed her eyes and winced at the pain that was sure to follow.

A sudden, forceful tug at her wrists pulled her body forward. Her head struggled to keep up with the abrupt change in direction. She was about to open her eyes when her face landed on a hard surface. Knowing that the floor couldn't possibly smell this good, she slowly opened her eyes and focused on a familiar tie.

"Miss Scott, are you all right?"

Slowly, Catherine removed her face from its present location.

"I think so," she answered as she brought her head up to meet her boss's intent gaze--only to cringe at the pain in her neck. She began rubbing at the injured spot without thought.

"Did you hurt yourself?" Mr. Reinhardt asked in concern.

"I think so, but I'm not really sure." Catherine wanted to put some space between them but didn't dare step back again. It seemed that Mr. Reinhardt was afraid of her falling as well. He had yet to take his arms from around her small waist. She was beginning to feel light-headed, but she wasn't sure if it was the crick in her neck or the smell of his cologne.

"Come this way. You need to sit down."

Catherine nodded and began walking alongside her boss, his right hand resting gently on her shoulder, guiding her through the office. Assuming that he had implied sitting down at her desk, she looked at him in question when he led her right past it. He just ignored her and continued across the open room.

When they came to the door of what was soon to be his office, he stood to the side and motioned for her to enter. Once inside, she sat down in the chair that he had pointed out. After seeing that she was seated comfortably, he sat down in the brown leather chair behind the desk and watched magnetically as Catherine rubbed at the back of her neck. When she finally looked up at him, she caught him staring.

"Are you okay, Miss Scott?"

"I'm sure I'll be sore for a couple of days, but considering the fall that I could have had, I guess I can't complain."

Catherine forced a smile, causing Mr. Reinhardt to wonder if she was always so optimistic. It would have indeed been a frightening fall, one that surely would have seriously injured her small frame.

"Well, I'm sure I'll be fine," Catherine said as she stood. Awkward wouldn't come close to describing how she felt sitting across from this man. "You probably want to get home." *I know I do.*

"Thank you for, um, catching me."

"You're welcome." Mr. Reinhardt stood and smoothed his tie with his hand. "The reason we had our collision was because I was attempting to stop you before you left."

"Was there something you needed?" Catherine asked. She couldn't help thinking that if this man asked her out, Megan would never let her live it down.

"It's about lunch," Mr. Reinhardt began as he stepped out from behind his desk. "I noticed that you ate with Miss Walker today." Catherine was about to ask if he was always so nosy when he answered her unspoken question.

"I think it's nice that you interact with your fellow colleagues, but don't turn your lunch break into the social event of the week. I'm asking everyone here, not just you, to keep it under an hour."

The whole time Mr. Reinhardt was speaking, Catherine wasn't paying full attention to his words. Rather, she was taking in each of his unique features. After all, she was a writer; she was supposed to notice things that others didn't. He certainly was handsome and well dressed, but one of the characteristics that stood out was his intimidating height. Although he was slightly over six feet, his straight posture gave him a look of authority that made him seem taller than he was.

When his words ceased, Catherine realized that she had only caught bits and pieces of what he had said.

"Yes, sir," she said, figuring it was a safe response to whatever he had been talking about. When he just nodded in return, she turned to leave. While he had been seated, Catherine had thought she had seen a hint of sensitivity in his eyes, but it had vanished the moment he had stood up. It was as if there was some switch in him that had activated, changing him from a gentle, attractive man into a power-hungry form in a suit.

When she came to the stairs, she turned briefly to ensure he hadn't followed her. Seeing that she was in no danger of bumping into him again, she began down the flight of stairs. As she made her way to her car she thought back over the day and all that had transpired. An overwhelming feeling came over her when she realized that it was only Monday, which meant she still had the rest of the week to endure Mr. Reinhardt's attempts to reform the office.

Seated once again at his desk, Lyndon Reinhardt fiddled with the fountain pen in front of him. Miss Scott had left his office more than ten minutes ago, but he still felt as if she were sitting in the room. Something in her mannerism intrigued him. She had been the first of his employees to speak to him with a smile on her face. Whether or not it was genuine, he had yet to find out.

The incident on the stairs had truly been an accident, but, if given the chance, Lyndon would gladly have rescued her again. As soon as the thought had formed, he pushed it aside. Miss Scott did not belong to him in any way. He knew better than to let his mind wander in that direction, even though she was indeed the most strikingly beautiful blonde that he had seen since he had moved to this small town.

Sighing, he stood and walked to the room's only window. The view was breathtaking--breathtakingly plain. There was no commotion. No honking horns and no wailing sirens. The town outside was peaceful. Lyndon was accustomed to the hustle and bustle of the city; the city was where he felt at ease.

He had not planned to move from his home to a no-name town in the country. He did plan, however, to be a lead editor, and taking this job had offered him a chance to make that rank years before he would have at the oversized, impersonal newspaper he had just left.

Making the most of his career was important to him, and he saw this as an opportunity to progress without stepping on anyone on the way up the professional ladder.

Hearing a sound behind him, Lyndon turned from the window to find Mr. Cady standing in the doorway.

"So, what did you think of your first day?"

Lyndon moved from behind the desk and motioned toward the leather chair. "Don't feel that you have to stand, sir. Have a seat. This office is, after all, technically still yours."

Mr. Cady smiled. Ignoring Lyndon's offer, he sat in the less domineering, less expensive chair that Catherine had recently vacated. Lyndon acknowledged the demonstration of humility and took the seat behind the desk. If not for the awkward encounter with

Miss Scott, he would have termed the first day as good as could be expected. He decided to answer Mr. Cady's question truthfully. "I think it went fairly well. Some moments were more interesting than others, but as a whole it went well."

"I'll be honest with you, Lyndon. The people of this office are spoiled. I'll be the first to admit it. As you can see, I'm not a very controlling man. I've let things become quite lax around here."

Lyndon smiled at the understatement.

"I understand that you may have a different way of doing things, but I ask that you not push these people too hard. They are, for the most part, responsible adults who work hard. I've never been demanding of them, but they've always produced only the best work for me."

"I respect your theory behind this 'hands off' method," Lyndon began, "but I come from a work force where rules are enforced, consequences are just, and authority is respected. I intend to lead a highly productive newspaper, not a coffee lounge."

"Then so you shall," Mr. Cady said as he stood. "I just wanted to let you know how things have worked here in the past. The future is up to you. I'll see you tomorrow."

With that he was out the door, and Lyndon once again found himself alone. Gathering his things, he decided to call it a day. And what an interesting day it had been.

After the traumatic transition Monday had afforded, Catherine was anxious to see what Tuesday would bring. To her surprise Mr. Reinhardt didn't so much as say hello to her. It was just as well considering their brief, but thorough, interaction from the day before. If it was left up to her, she gladly would never converse with him again. She would be perfectly satisfied going about her business, keeping all discussion limited to story assignments.

During the morning meeting, Catherine confirmed that Mr. Reinhardt had not changed overnight. Nothing had softened in his dictatorial style of leadership. Even Mr. Cady himself had hoped that the new editor would begin the day with a reformed attitude. But, as he had told Lyndon the day before, the whole office was his responsibility now.

Unlike Mr. Cady and the rest of the office, Catherine took the good with the bad. In her eyes, Mr. Cady had been ten times the boss Lyndon Reinhardt was. Although Cady's people skills were nonexistent, at least he had never looked at his employees as if they were a lesser form of life.

Regardless of her opinion of him, Mr. Reinhardt had been placed in her life in the form of her boss. The Bible told her to respect authority, whether it was the president, a police officer, or the editor of a small-town newspaper. Catherine's feelings, good or bad, didn't change God's Word. She had to remind herself of that very fact all day on Tuesday.

Wednesday's workday yielded no change with Mr. Reinhardt. He proved this by assigning Catherine two side stories along with her main article. Mr. Cady had never done anything of the sort. Nevertheless, Catherine did as she was told, which in turn caused her to fall behind. Rushing to finish, she was astonished when she turned her assignments. Mr. Reinhardt only pointed out all the mistakes he had found in them.

It was clear that he assumed himself to be greater and smarter than his subordinates. His actions had immediately begun to cause strife in the office. Catherine had thought the other employees' negative responses would gradually dwindle, but by Wednesday afternoon the remarks and comments were becoming overwhelmingly frequent.

The office as a whole was so negative that Catherine was more than happy to finish her work and head home. After a short dinner, she got into her rickety old car and began the twenty-minute drive to her church. She always found the mid-week Bible study to be interesting and enlightening, but tonight it was sure to be downright refreshing. She desperately needed to be in a positive atmosphere where she could share her burdens with others of her faith and then lift them to the Lord.

Upon entering the church Catherine was greeted by many familiar faces. The majority of the church body was made up of middle-aged families and a good group of senior citizens. She was only one of the handful of single individuals. The others were all college students.

Taking a seat she let out a sigh, wanting to release all of the stress of the busy day. She couldn't remember when she had been so mentally exhausted. Her day had been nothing but miserable. Megan had noticed her friend's frustration and had recommended that Catherine tell the boss exactly what she thought of him. For numerous reasons, Catherine had decided that was not the best course of action. For one, she wasn't the defensive type like Megan. Catherine would never pick a fight or even raise her voice to anyone, especially Mr. Reinhardt.

Mr. Reinhardt!

Catherine stared in astonishment at her boss, clad in a sweater and blue jeans, standing gawking down at her and looking equally surprised. Sure that this must be a mistake, Catherine searched for words but came up empty. What was he doing here? Some part of her had come here tonight to escape the pressures of the world. Now they stood before her in the form of this man.

"May I sit down?" Lyndon was the first to speak. His voice was so undemanding that Catherine didn't answer right away. It was as if he had been transformed. His change of attire had magnified the smooth lines of his face and brought out some softness in his dark eyes. But, above all, his voice was nothing like the man from the office. It was deep and soft as he spoke.

"Of course," Catherine answered automatically. "Have a seat, Mr. Reinhardt."

Lyndon gave her a tense smile and took a seat beside her.

"Please, call me Lyndon. Except when we're at the office of course." He waited for Catherine to pick up on his attempted wit, but she didn't give him so much as a smile. He decided to try again.

"Do you come here often?" he asked, trying to sort through some of the confusion they were both suffering from.

"Yes."

"How long have you been attending?"

"About four years."

Lyndon just nodded. Miss Scott wasn't being rude, but she certainly was not a fountain of information either. In fact, she seemed as if she wished he had never sat down beside her. Lyndon looked to the front of the room and, after verifying that the Bible study had yet to begin, inquired after the reason for Catherine's uncommunicative behavior.

"Is there something I've done to offend you, Miss Scott, or are you just afraid of me?"

Catherine was surprised by his question and took a moment to carefully choose her answer.

"Since you are here, I assume that we share a common belief, but you are still my superior and that position demands respect. Quite frankly, Mr. Reinhardt, *you* demand respect."

Lyndon blinked at her response. No one had ever said such a thing to him. It took a moment for her words to sink in. By then Catherine had turned her attention to the front of the room as the Bible study began. She was glad for the distraction. This man, handsome as he was, made her feel on edge. She felt as if every word out of her mouth affected the very welfare of her occupation and her standing at the office.

When the service had ended, Catherine immediately engaged in conversation with an older lady sitting in the next pew. The woman, Mrs. Cavanaugh, had an interest in writing and constantly questioned Catherine about her current story assignments. Catherine had always been willing to keep her up to date, but tonight she was more than happy to offer her information. In fact, she would rather do anything than be forced to speak to Mr. Reinhardt.

Seeing that Catherine wasn't going to give him the time of day, Lyndon decided to turn his attention to the other people who began introducing themselves to him. After numerous handshakes, he turned to speak to Catherine, only to find that she was gone. He smiled at her attempt to avoid him.

Lyndon found himself wishing that he didn't hold such a demanding position and title. He wanted to be kind--just as he wanted Catherine, along with everyone that he came in contact with, to see that he was capable of being a gentle and understanding human being. Unfortunately, with his current responsibility as editor, it was rather impossible to be so kind. The employees would see him as soft and walk all over him, just as they had Mr. Cady.

Sooner or later, Lyndon thought as he made his way home, *we'll finish this conversation, Miss Scott.*

Once inside her car, Catherine finally felt as if she could breathe. Lyndon Reinhardt. The *honorable* Lyndon Reinhardt had shown up in the most unlikely of places: her church! Was it possible that he was also a believer?

No. There's no way, she thought. He was too arrogant. Christians, at least the ones Catherine knew, were kind, meek, and patient. Mr. Reinhardt didn't meet any of the criteria.

Maybe he's a new Christian, she thought, continuing the conversation with herself. *Or, maybe he's just not grounded.*

Maybe you should stop judging him.

The last thought was something of a wake-up call for her. In all practicality, she had done nothing but focus on Mr. Reinhardt's faults since the first time she had seen him. It wasn't right to do, and she knew it. The hard part would be working with him every day and not gauging his every move, waiting for him to reveal his shortcomings.

Thursday morning again offered little change. Lyndon was still Mr. Reinhardt. The kind man Catherine had caught a glimpse of the night before had vanished, leaving behind only the same, unmistakable hierarchy.

For Catherine, a new day brought with it a new assignment. It was nothing spectacular, just a story about a high-school soccer team, but it did take up most of her day. For that she was thankful. A trip to the school and a few interviews kept her occupied until around one o'clock. She was whipping her story together, attempting to have it completed before the three o'clock meeting, when Mr. Reinhardt approached her.

"How's your story coming along, Miss Scott?" he questioned from behind her.

"It's just about finished," she answered, turning her body so as to form a barrier between her computer and the inquisitive Mr. Reinhardt. She was always self-conscious about people reading her stories before they were finished. It was as if it brought bad luck. It was all rather silly, considering she did not believe in luck. Regardless, she would prefer that no one read her articles until they were completed.

"Catherine?"

Catherine looked up at him, inwardly questioning his sudden informality. Had he not just told her the night before where he drew the line between respect and camaraderie? He had such a way of going from hot to cold so quickly with his ideas that Catherine could only stare at him in amazement.

"I'm sorry I didn't get a chance to catch you after the service last night," Lyndon said. "I was hoping we could finish our conversation some time."

"When?"

"How about after church on Sunday?" he suggested, thinking quickly on his feet.

Catherine was surprised. Not only because he wanted to talk, but also because he acted genuinely interested in attending her church.

"Mr. Reinhardt, I'm not sure I understand just what part of our conversation, or lack of, requires finishing."

"I just think we need to clear some things up."

Although she had no idea what her boss what talking about, Catherine just nodded, while inside she was screaming her refusal. Her mind swarmed with ideas. She tried with all her might to find a way of politely telling him that she did not want to have any kind of personal conversation with him.

"Well, whatever you have to say to me you can tell me right after the service on Sunday."

Catherine surprised herself with the icy tone in which her words had slipped out. She hadn't meant to be rude or sound angry. It was clear by the look on Lyndon's face that her tone, not her words, had left him speechless. He just stared down at her, studying her blue-green eyes, like he was trying to verify if she was indeed angry.

"I'll catch you after the service."

"Okay," Catherine agreed, thankful that he didn't seem to be shaken by her unruly outburst. "I probably should finish this story."

"Of course," he said with a charming smile. "I'll see you later."

That's just what I'm afraid of, Catherine thought as she watched him walk away.

Chapter Three

An escape was just what Catherine needed. Where to go and what to pack had been the least of her worries. She just wanted to be away from it all. As soon as work was over Friday afternoon, she was in the car and on the road. Her family lived an hour and a half away and to her that seemed like just the right distance for a getaway.

Once, when she was younger, she had vowed that she would never be happy living anywhere but home. The accident had changed her mind. When the dust had settled, she had left. The job as a journalist was just what she had wanted and needed. Much as she had hated to leave her family, she couldn't stand the memories that bombarded her heart when she was home.

It wasn't that way anymore. The wounds had begun to heal over the past four years. In fact, the pain of losing Jesse rarely ever crossed her mind. Whether or not it was because she had made herself forget in order to go on, was debatable. She had tried to move on though.

Staring at the road that would lead home, Catherine smiled at the sweet memories of the nineteen years that she had shared with her brother before his death. For so long it didn't seem real to her because she had been away at college when the accident had happened. It hadn't made losing him any less difficult, though.

At first it had been hard to go home and to see her family without Jesse. The grim reality of it all would rob her of the joy. But, now home was a safe haven rather than a place to avoid. The rest of her family had continued on with their lives. They had stayed in the same small town and had faced the future without their son and brother.

Catherine couldn't help but smile when her house came into view. It was an old farmhouse with lots of room--always full of love and character. Her father's farm sat just behind the large house. The barn's high arched roof and its sturdy, time-tested beams seemed to give even the house an appearance of strength and immortality.

Catherine had grown up in this house. Her parents, a teacher's daughter and a farmer's son, had married young and taken on the project of restoring a run-down house and business. Not very far along in the process, Catherine was born. Two years later she was followed by Jesse. The youngest was Leah. Although ten years separated her from Catherine, they were as close as two sisters could be and had the resemblance of twins.

Catherine tried to make it home as often as possible. It seemed that no matter how often she visited, her little sister always seemed to have grown up more.

Pulling into the driveway, Catherine placed her car in park and patted her dashboard, uttering a word of praise to her faithful means of transportation. She then grabbed her overnight bag, made her way to the back door and slipped inside. Leah was the first to spot her. She leaped from her seat at the dinner table and ran across the room with arms open wide.

"Katie!" the fifteen year-old exclaimed as she wrapped her arms around her sister. "Why didn't you tell us you were coming?"

"It was a rather impulsive decision," Catherine answered and smiled at her younger sister.

"Impulsive?" Evan Scott asked as he walked toward his older daughter. "You have never known the meaning of the word. My level-headed daughter never does *anything* impulsive."

Catherine smiled at the truthfulness in his words and gladly accepted the hug he offered. At last she turned to her mother.

"I'm sorry about the surprise, Mom."

Robin Scott shook her head and brought her daughter into her arms.

"You know we love having you here, Katie," she rebuked her with a smile, "whether or not it's a surprise."

"We're just having dessert. Come sit down with us," Evan said as he took the bag from Catherine and pulled out a chair for her at the table. "Tell us what you've been up to."

"Well, let me start by saying that I can only stay until tomorrow night. I have to meet someone after church on Sunday."

Leah's eyes lit up when she heard this.

"A date?"

"No, definitely not. It's my boss."

"You're meeting Mr. Cady after church?" Robin asked in confusion.

"No. Mr. Cady retired. Mr. Reinhardt is the new editor."

"What's he like?" Robin asked as she handed her older daughter a piece of apple pie.

"Truthfully, Mom, I came home to get my mind off work. Mr. Reinhardt is not going to follow me here."

Leah cast a glance at her mother and was met with a look that told her not to say another word on the subject.

"We won our soccer game yesterday," Leah told her sister in an effort to lighten the mood.

"Way to go. Did you score?"

"Katie, I'm the goalie," Leah stated cynically.

"Oh, I forgot."

"We're undefeated."

"Really? How many games have you played?"

"One."

Catherine laughed and took another bite of the delicious pie.

"How are things at church?" Evan asked. "Are you still teaching that class of wild animals?"

"No. Someone else decided to take the twos and threes challenge. I have this quarter off."

"Is it just me or does she sound disappointed?" Robin asked her husband and younger daughter.

"I was beginning to like the little rug rats," Catherine admitted.

"You never fail to amaze me," her father told her as he stood. "Grab yourself a cup of coffee and we'll continue this in the living room."

Catherine smiled at her father's wit. He knew full well that she hated coffee, or 'black poison' as she referred to it.

Leah followed Evan into the living room. As soon as they were out of earshot, Robin came over to Catherine and leaned against the counter.

"Tell me about Mr. Reinhardt."

"Mom," Catherine began to complain.

"Don't tell me that you don't want to talk about it. It's not like you to come home just to get away from something or someone. Now tell me."

Catherine let out a sigh and searched her mind for a place to begin.

"He's nothing like Mr. Cady, Mom. He's mean and bossy and demanding. He gives me three times more work than anyone else and always rushes to point out all of my mistakes. I guess he comes from the city and thinks that we are too *country* to know how to work."

"He sounds like quite an old ogre to me," Robin put in.

"That's just it. To look at him you would never expect what's hidden beneath his smooth face and dark hair."

"He sounds young."

"He is."

"And quite good looking."

"He is."

"And interested in you."

"He," Catherine stopped short and stared at her mother. "Definitely not!"

"Katie, you know how boys are in grade school. They pick on the girls they like because they feel it's the only way to get their attention.

Truth be known, grown men aren't much different. They may not pull your hair or trip you on the playground, but they'll find a way to get you to notice them. By the way you speak of Mr. Reinhardt, I'd say that he has your attention."

"But Mom, the man's appalling."

"I thought you found him attractive."

"It's not supposed to be about looks."

"You're right," Robin agreed. "It's based on respect and, above all, common ground in your faith."

"That's another problem."

"That he's not a believer?"

"No--that he is. At least, I think he is. He was at the Wednesday night Bible study."

Robin had no response to this. It was clear that her daughter was annoyed with this man, and at the moment, she had no advice to offer. When the table was cleared and the coffee had finished percolating, the women headed into the living room. Mr. Reinhardt wasn't spoken of again.

The organ played a prelude as Catherine entered the church on Sunday morning. As she took a seat she tried to sing the words in her head and concentrate on them. Halfway through the chorus, Lyndon took a seat in the pew in front of her.

"Good morning, Catherine."

"Good morning."

A rush of Lyndon's aftershave swept past her and Catherine told herself to breathe. He already had the advantage of his good looks. It would be much easier for her to dislike him if he didn't smell so good. Luckily for her, he didn't seem to force any type of conversation. Instead, he just sat silently waiting for the service to begin.

However, during the greeting time something that Catherine had never considered began to happen. It seemed every individual who shook her hand had a smirk on their face and a gleam in their eye directed not only toward her but to Lyndon as well.

At first she was angry, but she couldn't completely blame them for their assumptions. She was a relatively young female who, to the best of their knowledge, had never had a love interest of any kind. Seeing an attractive man, who was also relatively young, seated near her for the second time in a week, it was only fair of them to assume they were a couple.

Although the thought no longer made her angry, it did make her uncomfortable. She wanted to march up to the pulpit and announce that she was in no way associated with Lyndon Reinhardt other than that they worked together.

Instead, Catherine sat still and tried to remember the reason she was in church this morning. When her mind wandered to her new boss every three seconds, she would just keep reminding herself.

The moment that Pastor Wilson finished the closing prayer, Lyndon turned to face Catherine.

"So," he began.

"So, what?"

"Let's talk about your attitude. Tell me what your real problem is. And remember, we're not at the office. This is off the record."

"You sound like a psychiatrist."

"Very funny. Now speak."

"Now you sound like a dog trainer."

"Stop changing the subject, Catherine."

Lyndon rested his right arm on the pew between them. Her reaction was immediate.

"I would appreciate it if you kept your hands to yourself, Mr. Reinhardt," she demanded as she looked around to see if anyone had noticed the near contact.

"I didn't even touch you!"

"That doesn't matter. People are watching and I'm sure they already think we're…" Catherine stopped, unable to bring herself to the word.

"Dating?" Lyndon asked with a smile as he took his arm off the pew. "Well, back to our previous conversation. Are you still scared of me?"

"No. I'm not scared of you. I never was. I just don't like you," Catherine answered sarcastically.

"Why not?" Lyndon pretended to look crushed.

"Where do I start? You run the office like a prison work camp. You practically stand at the door with your stopwatch to ensure that no one is a second late. And then there's my personal favorite: you give me article upon article. I have my own assignments to do. Why do you single me out to overload with work?"

"Because, you're the--" Lyndon began.

"And why are you coming here? Do you honestly believe that you need to follow your employees?"

"I promise you, Catherine, that you are not the reason I am here. I'm looking for a church. So far I like this one."

"Okay, that answers one question," she stated, fighting the urge to cross her arms. "Now answer the other one."

"I was going to before you interrupted me. You're detailed and thorough. You do great work and seem to enjoy it. I thought you'd like the chance to expand a little."

Catherine nodded slowly and then stood.

"Where are you going?" Lyndon asked.

"Home."

"So, that's it?"

"I don't see why not," Catherine explained as she gathered her Bible and ever-present notebook. "You asked your questions and I answered. I asked my questions and you answered. That's all we needed to discuss. I'll see you this evening, Mr. Reinhardt, if you choose to come back."

Lyndon found himself seated alone and tried to think about the brief storm of conversation that had just transpired. For some reason, he couldn't remember a word Catherine had said. All he could recall was how flustered she had been when explaining her fear of letting people believe that they were dating. Somehow, that brought a smile to his lips. It seemed that he was getting through to Catherine Scott and he wasn't even trying.

A month had gone by before Catherine realized that Lyndon just might be serious about his reasons behind attending her church. He was at every service. Sometimes he would sit with her; other times he wouldn't. His actions and expressions always seemed sincere. When he spoke to her, the subject of work was never brought up and in those few fleeting moments, Catherine would begin to believe that if she were to peel away his exterior, he might possibly have a heart.

But, every Sunday was followed by a Monday. No matter how charming he had been on the weekend, Lyndon would never fail to become Mr. Reinhardt on Monday.

She tried to accept Lyndon's two-sided personality, but she could never get past the feeling that he was not going to work well as their editor. Something was going to have to change. Patience had always been one of Catherine's most admirable qualities, but it was beginning to dwindle with each passing day. By the end of the workday, she would feel like a bomb with a practically non-existent fuse.

She decided one evening that the best course of action would be drowning her work-related predicament in a movie. As she popped "Charade" into her DVD player, the front door opened. Megan kicked off her shoes and fell into the easy chair.

"Ah, 'Charade.' This is a good one," she said as she reclined the chair.

"Yeah," Catherine agreed with a sigh.

Megan took her eyes off the opening credits to look at her roommate. Catherine looked tired and distant.

"What's with you?" Megan asked but didn't bother waiting for an answer. "I bet Mr. *Rhino-heart* has you flustered doesn't he?"

She looked surprised. "Is that what everyone's calling him?"

"Everyone but you," she answered with a cheeky grin. "Word around the office is that he likes you, but I don't believe that rumor. I prefer the one about you two having a steamy intra-office affair."

Catherine laughed. "Well, he does have me flustered, as you put it, but not like that."

"How so?"

"Every day he gives me extra work and even some editing. Then, when I'm done with all of that, I have to research and write my own stories. For the first time in four years, I'm beginning to hate my job."

"You're right there with the rest of us. We hate him just as much as you do."

"I said I was beginning to hate my job, not Mr. Reinhardt," Catherine corrected her. "I don't hate him, and that's just the problem."

"How is that a problem?"

"If you could see the other side of him you'd understand."

"He has another side?"

"Yes. You've never seen him outside of work, have you?"

"No."

"I have. He's different. He's kind and soft-spoken—almost charming at times. He seems like two different men. One is the arrogant man that you see every day at the office. The other is a sensitive, and somewhat, normal human being," Catherine stopped and sighed. Venting, as good as it felt, didn't change anything.

In a way, she thought Megan had it easy. It took absolutely no effort at all to hate Lyndon as she said she did. Catherine, on the other hand, had the hard part. She had a witness to uphold in front of her co-workers. Any wrong action or word could turn them away from the God that she served. It was hard to like Lyndon when he was at work. She was always wondering how two completely different men could be living in one body.

"You know what you need, besides a new boss?" Megan asked.

"What?"

"A bowl of popcorn and a good movie, and since you're already watching a good movie, I'll get the popcorn."

Megan made her way to the kitchen and left Catherine to dwell on her thoughts. Slouching down a little further on the couch, she let her mind and body relax. When the movie was over, she would go to bed and not give work another thought until her alarm went off.

Five dollars to wash your own car! I could understand if someone came out and washed it for you, but why do I have to pay that much to wash it myself? Why am I washing this piece of tin anyway? It's November. It's going to get dirty just pulling out of the carwash. Washing it only draws attention to the rust and holes.

Five dollars! This car isn't even worth five dollars! And it's going to take a whole lot more than five dollars to fix it. I just wish I knew someone that I could trust to fix all these problems without running my bank account dry.

Catherine sighed as she dropped twenty quarters into the machine and picked up the nozzle. Just as the water began to shower out, she heard someone say her name. She turned quickly and stopped just short of spraying Mr. Cady with hot water.

"Sorry," Catherine raised her voice over the noise of the pressure washer. "I almost got you."

"I'm glad you didn't," Mr. Cady said, his voice equally as loud. "How've you been, Miss Scott?"

"All right. How about yourself? How's retirement?"

"Glorious. My wife and I are leaving after Christmas for a two-month vacation."

"Oh, how nice," Catherine said as she swept the nozzle back and forth across her car. In the four years she had worked for this man, she had never even known that he was married. He had always seemed like a content old bachelor to her.

"How are things at the office?"

It was the one question that she had hoped he would not ask. She stared at the soapy foam streaming down her car and tried to think of a polite way of telling him that he had made a terrible mistake choosing Lyndon Reinhardt as a replacement.

But how could she politely explain Lyndon Reinhardt or his actions? Was it even possible at all?

Without warning the spray of soap ended and was followed by high-pressure water. Catherine gripped the handle in frustration. Only half of her car was covered with soap.

Well, it looks like my car is only going to be half clean. Actually, half dirty is more like it.

Dirty. Just like Mr. Reinhardt's shenanigans. Her job was just like this carwash in some ways. It wasn't worth the money and it was fine until Mr. Reinhardt came along and the soap turned to ice-cold water.

Catherine began rinsing the soap off and stole a glance at Mr. Cady, who was still waiting for an answer to his inquiry.

"Things aren't going well, are they?" he asked, seeming to read her mind.

"It's just taking some time for all of us to adjust, that's all," Catherine answered, contemplating whether or not it was a lie.

"I know it's different, but try to remember that the reason Mr. Reinhardt seems like a power-hungry madman isn't because he is one—it's because I was too soft on you all. Most of the employees, including you, have never had an editor other than me. I am certainly not a good example to go by."

Catherine took a moment to think on his words. Coming from Mr. Cady, they seemed to have a sense of meaning, but she knew deep down that they weren't true. In her opinion, as well as everyone else's at the office, there was no excuse for Mr. Reinhardt's actions.

A buzzer sounded from the machine telling Catherine that the water would be ending in a matter of seconds. She quickly finished rinsing the clean half of her car and then placed the nozzle back in its holder. Turning to her former boss, she tried to think of something to say.

"You must blame me for hiring him, don't you?" Mr. Cady asked in a sad tone.

Catherine sighed and shrugged her shoulders.

"I don't blame you, Mr. Cady. You didn't know how he would run the office. Right?" she asked on second thought.

"Of course not," Mr. Cady assured her. "Well, I don't want to hold you up. I'll let you get back to your day."

"It was good to see you again."

"I hope things get better for you at the office, Catherine."

"Me, too. Goodbye."

After watching him disappear around the corner, Catherine got behind the wheel of her car. As usual, it took two tries to start it, but then she was on her way. She thought about how unlikely it had been to run into Mr. Cady. It was clear that he felt sorry for her and guilty that he was, in a way the cause of such upheaval in the office. But there was nothing he could do. He had no say at the office anymore.

Catherine felt trapped. It was as if she had been walking in a maze for the last month, only to turn a corner and find that she was back at the beginning again.

The moment that she stepped foot in her house, she made her way to the kitchen. After pouring a large glass of iced tea, she picked up the phone and dialed her parents' number.

"Hey, Mom."

"Katie! How are you?"

"All right. How are things there?"

"Good. I'm just baking for tomorrow's fellowship dinner at church. Your father and Leah are outside raking up what's left of the

leaves." Catherine could hear her mom open the oven door to take a peek. "Did you need to speak to one of them?"

"No. I actually called to talk to you."

"Is everything okay, Katie?"

"For the most part, I guess," she answered solemnly. "It's work. You know more than anyone how much I love my job, but lately work is the last place I want to be. It's one thing to have a boss who's so demanding, but the fact that Mr. Reinhardt calls himself a Christian just makes me angry."

"Have you spoken to him about this?"

"No. The only thing more confusing than Mr. Reinhardt is trying to talk to him."

"What do you mean by that?"

"He's a perfect fusion of clarity and miscommunication."

"Ah, Katie. You've always had a way with words," Robin said with a laugh. "You can take a simple concept and turn it into a collection of gibberish which I have no hope of understanding."

"And yet, Mr. Reinhardt says I'm a good writer."

"You are a great writer. When you sit down and scribble away in that notebook, the result is always amazing. I don't know where you got such talent, certainly not from your father or me. But we are so proud of your abilities."

"Thanks, Mom," Catherine said before taking a long sip of her iced tea. "Now what do I do about my boss?"

"Kill him with kindness," Robin said the phase that she had told her daughters many times over the years.

"Do you really think that will work?"

"I do. When he sees how nice you're being to him, despite the way he's treated you, he'll feel guilty and probably start acting better."

"Well, I suppose it's worth a try. Thanks for the advice, Mom. I'll keep you posted."

Moments later Catherine was off the phone. With the help of her mother she had formed a plan. Starting tomorrow, she would execute it.

Chapter Four

Catherine purposely showed up at church later than usual. It was imperative that Mr. Reinhardt arrive first. When she pulled into the parking lot, she nodded her head at the sight of his stylish, imported sedan, as if mentally marking a check on her imaginative battle plan.

Upon walking through the front door, Catherine was greeted by an usher. He smiled and handed her a bulletin. She made her way to the auditorium and found Mr. Reinhardt seated alone toward the back of the room.

"Good morning, Lyndon," she said, marveling at how strange his name sounded coming from her lips. "May I sit down?"

Lyndon could only stare at the beautiful woman addressing him. Her voice had never before sounded so sweet. What was even more surprising was that she had called him Lyndon. Surely, his name had never sounded so good.

"Have a seat," he offered, watching as she gracefully sat down and neatly placed her bulletin inside her Bible. "How are you today, Catherine?"

"I'm well. How has your weekend been so far?" Catherine asked, trying to sound genuinely interested.

"Quite busy, but I think I finally finished unpacking. Moving can be such a pain."

Catherine nodded and then asked a question she had been pondering.

"Why don't you work on the weekends? You are, after all, the lead editor."

"Well, I probably would have to if ours was a daily print newspaper, but since we only dispatch once a week, no one has to come in on the weekends unless they want to."

"Oh," Catherine muttered just as the organist began the prelude. She took the time to think over the last thirty seconds of conversation.

So far, so good, she thought and smiled to herself.

"Catherine?"

"In here," she called back to Megan from her bedroom. Seconds later Megan knocked on the closed bedroom door.

"Come in, Meg."

After slowly opening the door, Megan found her friend in a bathrobe and in front of her mirror, applying make-up.

"What's up?" Catherine asked as Megan sat down on her bed.

"Tim and I are going bowling. Want to come?"

"Who's Tim?"

"I met him at work. He's one of the new delivery men," Megan answered, seeming pleased that for once she didn't have to tell Catherine she had met him at a bar like all the others.

"Bowling sounds fun, but I already have plans."

"Do you, Catherine Scott, have a date?"

"No. I'm going to a writer's conference."

"On a Saturday afternoon?"

"Yes. It's only going on today."

"With whom are you going? I mean, you're way too dolled up to be going alone. Who's the lucky guy?" Megan coaxed her.

"If I told you, you'd kill me."

In a flash, Megan hopped from the bed and stood with her hands on her hips beside Catherine.

"Him? You're going with *him*? Are you out of your mind?" Her question was just short of an accusation.

"Yes, Meg," she answered calmly. "I am very much out of my mind."

"Honestly, what would possess you to do such a thing?"

"When I heard about the conference, I wanted to go, and it turned out that Lyndon wanted to go, too. We're just carpooling."

"*Lyndon*? I can't believe what I'm hearing, nor can I believe it's coming from you."

Megan walked vehemently to the door, turned back to Catherine and shook her head in disgust before walking out.

"Megan," Catherine called after her but was met with silence.

I can't make or expect you to understand this battle plan, Meg. I don't really understand it myself. Maybe it was a mistake, but it seems to be working. Lyndon's never treated me better than he has this past week. Is it worth the sacrifices, though? I don't want to lose my best friend in an effort to gain Lyndon's approval.

Catherine studied her image in the mirror and took in every detail. The look in her eyes told her that she was trying too hard. It was time to back off a bit. She had to make amends with Megan before she left the house.

Quickly, she slipped into the clothes that she had laid out on her bed. She made her way down the narrow hallway and checked Megan's room. Finding it empty, she walked to the living room and found Megan flipping through the channels from the couch.

Catherine took a deep breath, walked to the TV and shut it off.

"We need to talk, Meg," she stated kindly.

"I don't want to talk right now."

"Fine. Then we'll talk when I get back."

"If you get back," Megan huffed.

"What's that supposed to mean?"

"It means that you're taking an awfully big chance going out with him. I don't trust that creep any farther than I can spit on him."

"I don't want to point fingers," Catherine stepped out onto the proverbial thin ice, "but you don't seem to mind spending the night with a complete stranger that you met at a club."

Megan opened her mouth to defend herself but found that Catherine was right. Her shoulders slumped in defeat.

"I know you don't like him. From your viewpoint, I wouldn't either," Catherine said in an olive-branch tone. "But when he's not at work, he's actually nice to be around. Please, don't worry about me."

Megan remained silent for several seconds before looking up at Catherine.

"Okay. I still don't approve of it, but I have no reason not to. Let's not let Mr. Reinhardt come between us."

"It's a deal," Catherine agreed and made her way back to her room to finish getting ready. She was to meet Lyndon at the office in fifteen minutes and she knew better than to be late.

"So, where are you originally from, Mr. Reinhardt?" Catherine asked on their way to the conference.

"Please, stop calling me that. It's just Lyndon. You make me nervous when you sound so diplomatic. I'm from New Jersey," Lyndon replied. "It's nice there, right on the Pennsylvania border. It's not too crowded, but you're close enough to the city that if you ever need anything, you're right there."

"It must feel strange living in a town as small as Star Lake," Catherine said, almost feeling sorry for him. It must have been hard for him to leave his crowded city life just to come here for a job. But it was his choice after all, wasn't it? "What made you decide on this job, this town?"

"I've always wanted to be an editor. This seemed to be the best opportunity, so I took it."

"Are you glad you did?"

Lyndon turned to Catherine with a smile. A smile that she thought she knew the meaning of but hoped she didn't.

"It has certainly had its benefits."

Catherine told herself not to smile. Nowhere in her elaborate scheme did she allow for compliments, given or taken.

"What about you, Catherine? Did you grow up here in Star Lake?"

"No. My family is from Malone. It's about an hour and a half north of here."

"Oh, that's nice. So, you get to see them quite often?"

"I try to make it home as often as I can; usually once a month. It depends on how much I have to work."

"Is it just you or do you have brothers and sisters?"

"I'm the oldest. My sister Leah is ten years younger. Our brother Jesse was killed in a work accident when he was nineteen."

"I'm so sorry," Lyndon said genuinely. "How long ago did that happen?"

"About four years, now."

"Oh," Lyndon stated simply. He began putting the pieces together in his mind. She had said that she had been attending the church for four years, which happened to be the same amount of time she had been working for Mr. Cady. Now, he knew that her brother's death dated back that far. There was some underlying connection. Something had led her here at that time. But, it was none of his business. Not now, but maybe someday.

Silence fell on their conversation for a few minutes. Each individual's thoughts were on the words they had just spoken and on each other. Lyndon was the first to break the peaceful atmosphere.

"I understand that you and Megan Walker share a house."

"That's right. Meg and I have been friends since I moved here. We share the rent. It makes life much easier."

"I bet," Lyndon replied. "Do you carpool to work?"

"No," she answered, somewhat surprised that he didn't know that detail. After all, he seemed to keep all his employees on a tight leash. "We drive separately. Although we work in the same office and live in the same house, our ideas of fun extracurricular activities are contradictory."

"So, Megan doesn't share our faith," he stated.

Catherine didn't answer. She just stared at him a moment. The way he had pointed out that they shared the same love of God, the firmest foundation anyone could ever hope for, had made her look at him in a different light. For a moment she saw him not as her boss, but as a man. Not just any man, but a man her age who shared her faith. Perhaps he had been led to this place for a reason that involved her.

The very thought, and the possibilities it rendered, was sobering. Once again, she felt called upon to change the subject in her mind.

"Megan has a firm belief that all Christianity is boring. She'd rather live her life now, having what she calls 'fun', and deal with the consequences later."

Lyndon shook his head at Catherine's words. "It's obvious that she doesn't understand the breadth or reality of those consequences."

"You're right. I've lived my life as the best witness I feel possible, but now I believe that all I can do is pray for her."

"Then so will I," Lyndon offered. He looked over at Catherine, and for the first time since they had met, she didn't immediately look away. She locked her eyes with his, studying them so intently that he was afraid to blink for fear of losing the moment.

I wish you didn't despise me so much, Catherine, he thought to himself. *I'm starting to feel things for you that I've never felt for anyone. My motives are becoming so selfish where you are concerned. I didn't ask you to this conference to enrich your writing ability. I asked because I wanted to spend time with you and only you. I want to talk to you and listen to you. These feelings are against my rules, but part of me doesn't care.*

"This should be our exit." Catherine broke into his thoughts.

"I'm glad you pointed it out," Lyndon said as he switched lanes. "I probably would have driven right by it."

So he's distracted, Catherine thought victoriously. *My plan must be working. Maybe he's thinking of a way to treat me more like an equal, rather than a slave.*

"Thanks for inviting me to the conference and offering to drive," Catherine told Lyndon as they arrived back at the office. It was later than she had expected to be home, and she was starving. The conference had been enlightening, but other than some fresh fruit and expensive looking bottled water, it had offered nothing in the way of fulfilling refreshments.

"You're welcome. I'm glad you could go," Lyndon said as he pulled to a stop beside her car.

"I'll see you tomorrow," Catherine bid him goodbye and was opening her door to get out when Lyndon's voice stopped her.

"I would really," he began but paused indefinitely when she turned to him. For a moment her striking beauty robbed him of all his thoughts, and he forgot what he was going to say.

Catherine was just the opposite. Her mind was flooded with things that she wanted to say to Lyndon but couldn't.

Why can't you be like this all of the time, Lyndon? Why do you have to have two distinct personalities? If you were to act this nice all of the time, not just on the weekends, work would be so much easier.

Even as Catherine spoke the words to herself, she knew that if Lyndon changed his mannerism, work would indeed be easier; but her life, specifically not letting him into it, would become more difficult.

She studied his face and the smoky light in his eyes. His strong jaw line usually served as a reminder of how demanding he could be, but also drew her attention on many occasions. A slight shadow was forming on his cheeks, and she wondered if it bothered him that he, for once, wasn't clean-shaven. Finally, she realized that he had never finished his sentence.

"You would really what?"

Lyndon swallowed hard and tried to break the spell that her beauty had cast over him.

"I would really like to take you to dinner."

His words made her freeze like someone had just pressed pause. Only one thought dominated her mind.

Not part of the plan, Catherine. Not part of the plan.

"Are you buying?" she asked without thinking.

Lyndon laughed, flashing his bright smile.

"Yes, I'll buy. It's been a long day and I'm hungry. It's no fun eating alone. Please come. I can't take no for an answer."

"Can't or won't?"

"Can't. It's not humanly possible."

"I don't know, Mr... I mean, Lyndon," Catherine caught herself. "What would everyone from work think if they found out we had gone to dinner?"

"Who cares what they think," Lyndon lied. He did care. "We are two responsible, single adults." A chilling thought crossed his mind. What if she wasn't single? Just because she came alone to church didn't mean that she wasn't involved with someone back home.

"Do you have a boyfriend, Catherine?"

"As if it's any of your business."

"I'd like to make it my business," Lyndon said arrogantly.

Catherine rolled her eyes and climbed quickly from the car.

"Goodnight, Mr. Reinhardt," she managed just before she shut the door. "And, thank you for the ride."

Lyndon slammed the heel of his hand against the steering wheel as he watched her get into her car and drive away.

Bad move, Lyndon. You've got to take it slow or she'll never give you a chance. And you're going to need all the chances you can get.

"What was he thinking?" Catherine said aloud on her way home. For a moment, actually for the whole day, she had forgotten how arrogant and demanding Lyndon could be. She hated how inconsistent he was. If only he could be the 'weekend Lyndon' all of the time. Why did he think that she owed it to him to go out to dinner? Lyndon would no doubt want to talk about their disagreement tomorrow. Catherine made up her mind that if he asked her opinion of him, she would tell him. And she would be sure to leave nothing out.

Unfortunately for Catherine, she didn't get to voice her opinion of Lyndon on Sunday. He chose not to sit with her and barely said hello. Sunday evening brought the same result. It wasn't until Monday afternoon that their opposition came to a head.

Catherine was putting the finishing touches on her story, luckily the only one she'd had all day. She hadn't spoken to Lyndon, but every time he would walk past her desk she would hear the forced sound of Megan clearing her throat. She did her best to ignore Megan's verbal insinuations and Lyndon's unnecessary trips past her desk.

At last, she finished her story and turned it in to John, the copy editor. Once that was done, she walked briskly from his office and right into a familiar chest.

"Whoa! Maybe you need to slow down, Miss Scott," Lyndon suggested as he held her gently by the elbows.

"Yes, I should, Mr. Reinhardt, but I don't have time to." Catherine then stepped backward, putting a fair amount of space between them.

Lyndon frowned down at her and stood to the side.

"May I see you in my office?"

"Oh, no. Here it comes," Catherine said under her breath, but loud enough for him to hear.

They made their way down the hall, across the open room filled with computers, and into his office. Lyndon closed the door but left the shades open. People had enough to talk about.

"What is wrong with you?" Lyndon demanded as soon as he turned from closing the door.

"Wrong with me?" Catherine asked aghast. "The only problem I have is *you*."

"Oh, is that right? Why don't you elaborate on that?"

"Fine. I am so sick of your split personality!"

"What in the world is that supposed to mean?" Lyndon asked.

"Saturday and Sunday you are fun to be around. You're soft-spoken and considerate, but as soon as you set foot in this office, you become somebody completely different." Catherine was shocked by her own words. She never argued with anyone. This was new territory for her.

"I have a job to do. I can't go around here being everyone's buddy. I'm the boss. I need to act like one."

"I understand that, but we're supposed to be setting an example for everyone here. They're not going to want anything to do with our faith if they all despise you."

"Then what would you suggest? You seem so full of answers," Lyndon said with his arms crossed.

"Just loosen up a bit. You can be in control without being mean."

Lyndon walked slowly over to his desk and leaned against it. He was silent for a few moments.

"Believe it or not, I care what you think. I'm not used to doing anything someone tells me to, but if this will put us back on good terms, then I'll try it."

Catherine smiled at his defeat, but Lyndon raised his hand.

"On one condition," he started. "If I act less mean, as you so gracefully put it, can we be friends outside of the office?"

"If that's what you want."

"Well, I still really want to take you to dinner. Are you free tonight?"

"Yes."

"Yes, you're free or yes, you'll go with me?"

"Both."

"Okay. Do you want me to pick you up, or do you want to meet somewhere?"

"Let's meet. Is seven too late?"

"No. That's perfect," Lyndon said as he walked over to the door and opened it for her. "Do you like Roma's?"

"Yes. I love their food."

"All right. Seven at Roma's," Lyndon recited with a smile. He watched Catherine walk back to her desk and gather her things. For him, seven o'clock couldn't come soon enough.

"I'm sorry you burned your tongue, but it did give me the best laugh of the evening watching you elegantly spit out your food," Catherine told Lyndon as they made their way to their cars. Dinner had been wonderful, as had the consistent conversation.

"I'm glad you enjoyed that. Remind me to point and laugh the next time that you put a forkful of scalding spaghetti sauce in your mouth." Lyndon pretended to be perturbed, but Catherine knew that he also found the incident very funny.

When they reached her car, Catherine turned to look up at him. His dark hair reflected the streetlight, and she could see that he was smiling.

"Aren't you glad you came?" he asked.

"I am. It's really nice to hang out with this side of you."

"Good. Would you like to see a movie with 'this side of me' on Saturday?"

"I don't know. Last Saturday was fun but ended in disaster," Catherine admitted.

"I'll be on my best behavior."

"Okay. I probably can manage it. Thanks for dinner. I'll see you tomorrow," Catherine said as she got into her car.

"Are you sure this thing will get you home?" Lyndon asked as he tapped the roof of her car.

"I'll be fine."

With that, Catherine pulled away. She wasn't mad at him, but she couldn't help feeling that he thought he was better than everyone in the town because he had a prominent job and a nice car. She didn't want to judge him, but he did seem to have an issue with pride. Overall, he was nice, but he did not seem to be the strong man of faith that she was hoping to marry someday.

You shouldn't be dating him if you don't think he's marrying material, Catherine.

I'm not dating him, she told the voice in her head. It was a lie, and she knew it. Not on her part. She felt that she wasn't dating Lyndon, but also knew that it was wrong to let him believe they had a future. In her opinion, she was just killing him with kindness. It appeared as if she were doing a first rate job.

It didn't take long at all for Catherine to discover that Lyndon was indeed trying to change the way he ran the office. The morning meetings were much less uptight. Coffee was no longer forbidden in the conference room, and even Lyndon himself was seen bringing in a cup or two. Several glances of awe were shared around the table when he took a seat at the head of the table instead of standing.

When Catherine's assignments were given, she was always rewarded with a slight smile. She couldn't help but smile back. When she did, Megan proceeded to nudge her beneath the table, causing Catherine to turn and scowl at her.

It was nothing but a relief to see Lyndon doing so well. It seemed as if everything Catherine had worked so hard for was coming together at last, but she was wrong. Lyndon was trying to change and doing his best, but he hadn't worked at all on his underlying problem: pride. It was still there and as destructive as ever.

One week after his supposed transformation Lyndon proved to Catherine, as well as everyone at the office, that he hadn't changed at all.

Catherine arrived at work fifteen minutes early as usual. She was becoming accustomed to being greeted by a cheerful Lyndon and this morning was no different. Everything was normal up until the moment that Megan quietly made her way into the conference room halfway through the morning meeting.

Upon its conclusion, when everyone went their separate ways, Megan leaned over to her best friend and whispered forcefully to her.

"Why didn't you wake me up before you left?"

"Was I supposed to?"

"No, but didn't you think it a little odd that I wasn't up when you left?"

"For all I knew, you could have called in sick," Catherine reasoned. "I'm sorry, Meg."

"It's not your fault," she said, this time without as much steam. "I stayed out way later than I should have," Megan explained as both women sat down at their desks.

"Miss Walker. I'd like to see you in my office," Lyndon said from behind them, surprising both of the women.

Catherine couldn't help but feel sorry for Megan as she watched her obediently follow Mr. Reinhardt into his office. No doubt he would sit her in the time-out chair and make her endure his entire spiel about not being late and how disrespectful and unprofessional it is.

Several moments passed before the sound of a slamming door startled Catherine. She looked up to see Megan stomping across the room. Her eyes were ablaze with anger. Her face looked almost blue, as if she had been holding her breath. Catherine stood and walked to meet her at her desk, where she was grabbing her purse.

"Where are you going?"

"Home," Megan answered between clenched teeth.

"Home? Why?"

"Your little *boyfriend* just fired me!"

"He did what?"

Megan repeated her words to Catherine, only this time she threw in some choice phrases to describe her now former boss. After that, she whirled around and left the office. Catherine was left standing alone and feeling furious with Lyndon. She looked over at his office door. It was still closed from Megan's abrupt exit. With her eyes narrowed to give her that 'ready for battle' look, she walked to his office and without knocking opened the door.

Lyndon looked up from the papers on his desk in surprise.

"Ever heard of knocking, Cat?"

"Don't 'Cat' me," she quipped. "Do you have any idea how big of a mistake you've just made?"

"Catherine," he began smoothly in defense, "please try and remember that I am the boss."

"Dang-it, Lyndon, I'm not a child. Don't talk to me like I'm a little girl!"

"I have to do what's best for this company."

"I think that's a lie," Catherine countered him. "I think you're so dependent on your position that as soon as you feel threatened, you fire an honest, hard-working woman just to give your ego a boost. That is so low."

"You're wrong," he accused her as he stepped close to her and pointed his finger in her face. "You're wrong, and you're out of line. I fired her because I can't have all of my employees thinking that it's okay to show up late, play on the computer all day, and turn in poor assignments. I made it perfectly clear from Day One that I wouldn't tolerate it. I didn't fire her because she's your best friend or because it makes me feel good about myself. I don't play favorites, Catherine."

"So, you'd fire me if I showed up late?"

Lyndon hesitated for a moment. "Yes. I would if that's what was best for the company," he answered, still standing within a foot of her. He could see she hadn't expected that response.

"Well, perhaps I should be looking elsewhere for a job."

It was the kind of declaration that she would have loved to scream at her boss, but the words came out in a controlled decibel, causing Lyndon to freeze.

She couldn't be serious, could she?

"Please," he begged her in the smoothest voice possible, "don't say that. I need you here. I need you on my team."

"Prove it. Give Megan her job back," Catherine offered, but Lyndon just shook his head.

"I can't do that."

"Fine." She shrugged her shoulders and turned to leave.

"Wait!" Lyndon took her wrist and whipped her back around to face him.

"Why should I?" she demanded.

Lyndon had no answer but knew that he couldn't let her leave like this. Somehow, he had to convince her to stay and reconcile.

He stared down at her intently. Her face was lit up with furry, and her eyes looked greener than ever before. Her lips, which were usually beautifully curved in a smile, were instead tight in anger, causing Lyndon to lose all concentration.

Before she could react, Lyndon lowered his head and firmly covered her lips with his own.

Chapter Five

Catherine, completely shocked, tried to back away. Lyndon just gripped the back of her arms and pulled her into another kiss. This one wasn't as forceful. For a moment, Catherine forgot what she was doing and who she was kissing. She lost herself in the warmth of his mouth and the slow tightening of his arms.

It felt so good to have Lyndon's arms around her.

Lyndon!

Placing both her hands on his chest, Catherine pushed away and stared at her boss in shock. He seemed in shock as well not--that he had kissed her, but that for a moment she had kissed him back.

"What the heck are doing?" Catherine asked in a breathless tone.

"I don't honestly know, but I like it. I think you do too," Lyndon said, not missing the rush of pink in her cheeks.

Catherine wanted to reprimand him but couldn't find the words. She just stared blankly at his tie and rubbed her forehead. A noise from outside the office caught her attention. Her jaw dropped when she saw that the door, along with the window shades, was still open, allowing the entire office to observe their foolish display.

In a normal human reaction, she walked quickly over to the door and shut it with a bang. Then she turned to Lyndon.

"I cannot believe you just did that!"

"I'm sorry that everyone saw it. I know it's against policy."

"I don't understand you, Lyndon."

"What's not to understand?"

Catherine let out a breath of frustration.

"One minute you're yelling at me and the next you're kissing me senseless."

"Senseless?"

She ignored him and went on.

"All week you've been a perfect reflection of understanding and then you pull a stunt like this."

"Stunt?" Lyndon asked, assuming she was speaking of the kiss they had shared.

"Firing Meg," she clarified. "Lyndon, regardless of her short comings she's one of your best employees. Do you know how hard it's going to be to replace her?"

"I guess I didn't think about that," Lyndon admitted honestly.

"I guess not. You don't think about a lot of things."

For a moment they both were silent. Lyndon was worriedly running his fingers over his chin, staring down at the floor in deep thought.

"What are you going to do?" she asked.

"About us?"

"About Megan."

"What's done is done, Cat. I can't take it back."

"Okay, I'm confused. Are you talking about this little charade," she waved her hand across the room, "or about Meg?"

"Both."

"Let's get one thing clear, buddy, if you ever want to see me on any type of non-professional basis, you're going to have to prove how much it really means to you."

"How?"

"By giving Meg her job back."

"Catherine, please don't make me choose between you and this job," Lyndon begged her as he took a step forward. Catherine raised her hand to stop him.

"Don't get any closer. If you touch me again without permission, you're going to regret it," Catherine told him firmly. "As for you choosing me or work, I'd think the choice would be quite simple. If you choose work over me, you'll no longer have me as an option."

"Don't bribe me like this," Lyndon warned.

"I'm going to give you some time to think it over," Catherine told him in an unwavering tone. "If Megan's not back here by the week's end, don't plan on my being here either."

Leaving him speechless, she stormed from the room and made her way to her desk. It was hard not to notice the stares she was receiving, but she did her best to ignore them and focus on her assignment. It was no use, though. Every time she tried to concentrate, her thoughts detoured to the scene in Lyndon's office.

It was selfish, as well as inconsiderate of Megan's feelings, to be dwelling on the ordeal with Lyndon instead of the predicament in which Megan now found herself. Catherine found no help for it, though. She was mad at her boss; she couldn't deny it, but for some reason she kept feeling her face heat each time she thought back over the incident.

Catherine came home to an empty house later that afternoon. Megan's car wasn't there, and Catherine could only imagine where she was or what she was drinking.

After taking a long shower to ease away the tensions of the day, Catherine went to work on dinner. She was standing at the counter in her bathrobe with her damp blonde hair hanging past her shoulders when the front door opened. Megan stepped inside and made eye contact with her roommate who immediately tried to reconcile.

"I don't want to talk about it," she told Catherine as she walked right past her, leaving behind the unmistakable smell of liquor. The ringing of the doorbell captured both women's attention.

"Are you expecting someone?" Catherine asked.

"No, but I'll get it. You're not even dressed," Megan offered as she made her way over to the door, opened it and then slammed it shut.

"Who was that?" Catherine asked.

"Him."

"Meg, just hear him out," Catherine pleaded with her as she walked to the door, forgetting her appearance. Opening the door, she found Lyndon still standing on the steps.

"What do you want?"

Lyndon tried not to stare at the way she was dressed. He had never seen her without her make-up and her hair so disheveled. She looked absolutely beautiful.

"I need to talk to Megan."

"I've got nothing to say to you," Megan called from behind Catherine.

"Megan," Lyndon began as he squeezed past Catherine and entered the house uninvited. "I want to apologize about today and offer you a second chance."

"You're a little too late, Mr. Reinhardt. I wouldn't come back if yours was the last job on earth! I can't work for someone so inconsiderate. I have no idea what Catherine sees in you. I think you're an appalling excuse of a man!"

Megan turned, stomped down the hall, and slammed her bedroom door for emphasis.

"I tried, Cat. You can't say I didn't try."

"Honestly, I didn't think you would do that much. I'm proud of you."

"I want to apologize to you, too. I was out of line by kissing you. Next time, I'll be sure to ask your permission."

"What makes you so sure there'll be a next time?"

"Mark my words," he began as he made his way to the door. "There will most definitely be a next time. Will I see you at the office tomorrow?"

"I suppose you'll have to wait and see," Catherine challenged him, but her eyes told him that she'd be there. "Goodbye, Lyndon."

"Goodbye."

Lyndon was halfway down the sidewalk when Catherine called after him.

"Lyndon?"

"Yeah?"

"How'd you know where I lived?"

Lyndon smiled sweetly and gave her a wink.

"I'm the boss, remember? I know everything." He turned to leave and called out over his shoulder: "Nice bathrobe, by the way."

Things were different at the office without Megan, but in a way, her leaving had been a turning point for Lyndon. His weekend personality was beginning to become the norm. The employees were much less disgruntled, and the office as a whole took on a laid-back atmosphere. Everything seemed to be on the right track and it was all because of Catherine. Lyndon had no other choice but to treat his employees like royalty if he wanted to hang on to her. No one had ever had such control over him.

Every time he even considered being domineering, she would give him her "you know better" look. She made it perfectly clear that if he wanted her as an employee and a friend, he had to be on his best behavior at all times.

The issue of friendship was the subject of many of their conversations. Lyndon had told her that he wanted to be a permanent fixture in her life, but time and time again she tried to convince him that they weren't compatible.

Catherine honestly believed that it was true, but in the back of her mind she constantly wondered if she were making a mistake by not letting Lyndon into her life. She wasn't getting any younger, and she did want a home and a family. Those were two things that Lyndon could give her.

Robin called one Friday evening to see if her daughter would care for some company over the weekend. Catherine, although she would have to cancel her usual Saturday evening 'date,' was more than happy to hear that her mother and sister were coming. Her father had to stay behind with the farm, but he knew that the women would have a wonderful time, even if he couldn't be there.

Catherine was thankful that her mother and Leah were coming because it would provide her with an opportunity to not only explain her 'relationship' with Lyndon, but to ask their advice about it as well.

When she called Lyndon to tell him that she wasn't going to be able to make it to their 'date,' he was understanding and even asked if he could have the pleasure of meeting her mother and sister.

"That depends," she had told him.

"Depends on what?"

"On whether or not they kill me when I tell them we've been spending time together."

"That's reason enough for me to meet them. They'll have no problem once they see how wonderful I am."

"The sad thing is that you believe it," Catherine told him before they hung up.

Robin arrived in Star Lake slightly earlier than required, a trait she had passed on to all three of her children. Catherine had spent most of the morning cleaning the house and picking up groceries. Megan slept in late and had left the house without so much as a goodbye, leaving Catherine alone to greet her mother and sister.

The three women sat around the kitchen table for some time discussing the events of the past few weeks. Robin related her plans for Thanksgiving dinner and orchestrated all of the details with Catherine. For the most part, the conversation was placid.

Catherine quickly filled them in on the news from church, mentioning that Lyndon had been attending regularly.

"Who's Lyndon?" Leah questioned her older sister.

"My boss."

"You got *another* boss?"

"No. It's the same one."

Catherine saw that Leah's confused look was begging for an explanation.

"Are you telling me that you're dating the same man you couldn't stand a month ago?"

"We're not dating, Leah," Catherine tried to explain, but was met with an unbelieving look. It was time to tell the whole story.

"I need to explain this to you both, so hear me out. When Lyndon came here he…he turned the office upside down with his work tactics. In the beginning, I couldn't stand it. Not only because he seemed to single me out with more work than anyone else, but also because he brought absolute distress to the office. For a while, I considered looking somewhere else for work."

"Through church, I began getting to know a different side of him. I could see the promise of a great editor, but his pride and arrogance left no room for people skills. So, for the sake of my co-workers and myself, I took matters into my own hands. I may have been wrong in doing so, but I let him know just what his problem was."

"Things were better for a while. He seemed to be trying harder for the sake of winning me over. Maybe that's wrong too, but it worked. Then everything crumbled when Lyndon fired Megan. When I confronted him about it, he told me that he had a position to uphold and that he had fired Meg for the good of the company. I told him flat-out that if he ever wanted a relationship of any kind with me, he would have to give Megan her job back."

"Later that afternoon he stopped by here to talk to Meg, but she told him she didn't want her job back. Since then he's been nothing but charming."

"Are you really interested in him or are you just toying with him to keep the office running smoothly?" Leah asked.

"A little of both, I'm sorry to say."

"Do you think that he's in love with you?" Robin inquired.

"I don't think I'd call it love but he's certainly interested. Do you think seeing him is wrong, Mom?"

"Spending time with him isn't wrong, Katie. If he thinks you're dating, then you have a problem."

"I've told him that we're not compatible, but he still wants to spend time with me."

"Well, I think it's okay, as long as he knows that you just want to be friends," Robin concluded.

"Who knows? Maybe you'll fall for him over time," Leah, the hopeless romantic of the family, put in.

Catherine knew that it would never happen, but she also knew better than to say never.

"Lyndon, I'd like you to meet my mom, Robin, and my sister, Leah."

"It's a pleasure to meet you both," Lyndon said as he shook both women's hands on Sunday morning. Robin gave him a look of approval, and Leah stared at him like she had never seen such a good-looking man in all her fifteen years.

After the introductions were made, all four took a seat and waited for the service to begin. Catherine was thankful that Lyndon didn't lean over to talk to her at any time during the hour. She never would have heard the end of it from Leah.

Directly after the service, he wasted no time in asking the women to lunch. Catherine wanted to object, but Robin was accepting his invitation before she could speak.

"You could have asked if I wanted him to go, Mom," Catherine said later as they made their way to the car.

"You spend every other waking moment with him, so I just assumed that you wouldn't mind."

"I certainly don't mind," Leah interjected. Robin and Catherine stopped walking and turned to the youngest member of the Scott family for an explanation.

"What?" Leah asked with a smile. "He's the most amazingly gorgeous man I have ever seen, Katie. I think you're crazy for not being crazy for him."

"There's more to it than good looks, Leah," Catherine explained. Robin nodded in agreement, and all three of them piled into the car.

Lunch was a huge success on Lyndon's part. He was attentive to the conversation and asked enough questions to make everyone feel included. Leah enjoyed this more than the delicious food.

Catherine warned Lyndon with a look of steel when, leaving the restaurant, he placed his hand on the small of her back to lead her through the door. Robin and Leah both saw the act and shared a smile.

Once in the car, the conversation revolved around Lyndon. Robin commented that he was not only good looking, but considerate as well.

"Therein lies the problem," Catherine began. "I can't convince Megan that he's actually a sensitive human being because she only saw him at work. Yet, I can't convince you that he's incorrigible because you've never seen how forceful he can be."

"Forceful?" Robin repeated. Seeing the slightest color rise in Catherine's face, she probed. "Please, elaborate on that."

"Mom,"

"Katie, I'm your mother, and I don't like the word *forceful* being associated with the man my daughter's seeing." Robin's blue-green eyes were narrowed and stern. For Catherine, it was like looking in a mirror.

"Mom, it's nothing, really."

"Is it? Was it nothing I saw when you two went through the door leaving the restaurant?"

"Okay, if you have to know," Catherine said and took a quick glance at Leah sitting patiently in the back seat. She hated to relate the story in front of her impressionable fifteen year-old sister, but it seemed that she had no choice.

"The day that he fired Megan, I went into his office to confront him about it. We argued, and I told him that I was going to leave to find work elsewhere. I think it scared him into finding a way to make me stay. When I turned to leave, he stopped me."

"Did he hurt you? If he laid a hand on you..." Robin's voice trailed off.

"He kissed me," Catherine answered softly, feeling her face heat in embarrassment.

"Kissed you? What kind of kiss?"

"Mother!"

"I'm sorry. That was kind of personal. Have you kissed him since then?"

"No. I told him to never do it again without my permission."

"I'm proud of you, Katie, for laying down the law. Most girls your age wouldn't even consider resisting a man that handsome."

"I know I wouldn't," Leah said from the back seat.

"Leah!" Robin scolded, trying to hold back her smile. When she looked at Catherine, who was just shy of laughing, she couldn't hold it in any longer. All three women shared a good laugh. It was the perfect note to end on.

Leah and Catherine were still awake long after Robin had turned in on Sunday night. Catherine knew that she had to work in the morning and Leah was leaving early enough to be on time for school. But, it was so nice to be near each other that neither of them could say goodnight.

"Now that Mom's not here, tell me what it was like," Leah prodded her sister.

"Kissing Lyndon? It wasn't any different than kissing anyone else."

"Work with me here, Katie. You're talking to someone who's never had that pleasure."

"Well," Catherine began with a sigh, "at first it's awful having someone you don't particularly care for hold you tightly. I felt like I couldn't escape. The human body is like a live wire; one touch and it sends a shock through you with enough force to take your breath away. For a moment I forgot that I was kissing Lyndon. Luckily, I didn't forget for very long."

"Oh, it's so romantic how you couldn't stand him at first and now you're dating him," Leah sighed breathlessly.

Catherine shook her head. "We're not dating. If you like him so much, maybe you should marry him."

Leah laughed.

"Honestly, Leah. Do you think I should settle for someone like him?" she asked in a sobering tone.

"Christian men are hard to find. I'd fish while they're biting. Maybe you could learn to love him if you overlook his faults."

"What if his faults are un-overlookable?"

"I can't help you there. Just keep praying about it."

Catherine scooted over on the couch and hugged her sister tightly.

"You're my hero, Leah. You're becoming a remarkable young woman. Jesse would be so proud of you."

"Do you still miss him?" Leah asked when she could once again see Catherine's face.

"Yes. I always will. Most of the time, I'm just sad that he's gone, but sometimes I still get mad that he had to be the one to die that day. I just remind myself that it was all in God's plan."

The room was silent for a moment.

"Do you think that we should call it a night?" Leah asked.

"I suppose so. Make sure you don't wake Mom up when we go to bed."

"I won't," Leah assured her with a smile. Catherine was thankful for the weekend. Not only did had she had a wonderful time with her mother and sister, but she had also attained some useful advice, which she was sure to need.

"Oh, come on, you piece of tin," Catherine told her car as she turned the key for the fifth time. "Don't let me down." Still the car made no effort to start. She gripped the steering wheel and laid her head against it. "You can't give up on me now."

Finally, she gave up and got out. Opening the door and closing it gently, so as not to break it off its hinges, she made her way inside to call Lyndon.

"Hello?"

"Oh, good you're still there."

"I was just walking out the door. What's up?"

"My car won't start. Do you think you could swing by here and pick me up?"

Five minutes later, Catherine was fastening her seatbelt in his car.

"I really appreciate this, Lyndon. I hope it doesn't make us late."

"Then I'd have to fire myself," Lyndon said as he pulled out of her drive.

"And me, too," Catherine reminded him.

"That's not necessarily a bad thing."

"What?" Catherine's mouth hung open in astonishment.

"The last time that I fired someone, I was rewarded with a very enjoyable experience." Lyndon looked over at her with a grin. When they came to a stoplight, he took his right hand off the steering wheel and held it between them. Catherine looked down at his smooth palm and then up at him. His face was undemanding and gentle, as if he had all the time in the world.

"May I hold your hand, Catherine?"

As much as Catherine wanted to take a few minutes to consider his request, she found herself answering immediately.

"I'm sorry, but it wouldn't be fair. I can't let you believe that I have the same feelings for you that you do for me. Not now at least, anyway."

Lyndon rested his arm on the center console and let out a deep sigh.

"Do you think you might care for me someday?"

"I don't know."

Catherine couldn't think of anything else to say. She couldn't lie to him. A change in subject seemed to be the best answer.

"What am I going to do about my car?"

"Do you know what's wrong with it?"

"If I did it wouldn't need to be fixed, would it?"

"Oh, right. Well, we can get someone to tow it over to Carey's while we're at work," Lyndon suggested.

"No way. No one is touching my car until I have a nice, long talk with them. They are going to give me an exact quote on how much it's going to cost, and I'll make it perfectly clear that I'm not paying a penny more than that."

"Wow! You are tight when it comes to your car."

"I have to be. My job is more of a hobby than a money-maker."

Lyndon felt guilty that he had accused her of being stingy.

"Don't worry. Carey's a Christian. He won't take your money and run," Lyndon assured her.

Catherine still didn't like the thought of going to see a mechanic, but her reasoning had nothing to do with money. It went so much deeper than that.

"How do you know this guy?"

"We met at the men's conference last month. He told me to stop by if I ever needed any work done. I took my car over to get winter tires put on, and he didn't charge me a penny more than he said he would."

"I guess if you recommend him he can't be too bad," Catherine said as the office came into view.

"What is it with you and your fear of mechanics? It's like you're going to get your teeth pulled."

"I've never met one I can trust."

"You will this afternoon. I'll call the tow truck and take you to Carey's right after work, okay?"

Catherine nodded and thanked him. If this mechanic turned out to be a gold-digger, she was going to kill Lyndon.

Chapter Six

When Catherine and Lyndon pulled into the small parking lot later that afternoon, Catherine almost cried at the sight of her car parked all alone in the corner. She stood staring at it for a while before Lyndon leaned close and caught her attention.

"Don't be shy, Cat. It's this way."

The sound of air tools and pounding welcomed them once inside the door. No one was in the office, so Lyndon stepped around the corner into the bay. The pounding immediately stopped.

"I'll be right there," a man's voice called.

Lyndon walked back into the small office, which consisted of a desk and three chairs. Right away he noticed Catherine's face. She was pale and looked like she was facing her own execution. Her arms were crossed in front of her as if she was hugging herself. It gave her the appearance of an insecure teenager.

"It's okay," Lyndon assured her as he placed his arm around her waist and pulled her close. "I don't understand this fear of yours, but I'm right here for you. I'm not going anywhere."

Catherine looked up at Lyndon. His face was within inches of hers.

"That's undoubtedly the nicest thing you've ever said to me."

Lyndon peered down into her beautiful eyes, eyes that gave away her every emotion. He was sure they were telling him that she cared for him. The urge to kiss her was so strong--she looked so vulnerable. He wanted to kiss her long and hard to prove to her that she needed him.

Catherine couldn't look away from Lyndon. For a moment she felt so secure with his arm around her, and for just as brief a moment, she wanted to kiss him again. The sound of footsteps bluntly halted her emotions. Feeling foolish, she tried to back away, but Lyndon wouldn't release his arm from around her waist.

"Lyndon! How've you been?" the mechanic asked as he entered his office.

"Fine. And you?" Lyndon finally released his hold on Catherine to shake the other man's hand.

"I'd shake your hand but I wouldn't want you to get your suit dirty. How's work been?"

Catherine watched the two men as they conversed. From the outside it appeared as if they had nothing in common. Lyndon was still in his suit and tie while the other man's blue jeans and t-shirt were plastered with grease. His face had clearly not been shaven in a few days, but his eyes were the deepest blue that Catherine had ever seen.

"Carey, I'd like you to meet Catherine. She's one of my employees and goes to the church I've been attending. Catherine, this is Adam Carey, the trustworthy mechanic I was telling you about."

"It's nice to meet you, Catherine."

For the first time since Adam had entered the room, he made eye contact with the most beautiful woman to ever step foot in his office. There was something so familiar about her, but he couldn't put his finger on it.

"Have we met before?"

"Not that I know of," Catherine told him, although she also had a feeling that they knew each other.

"Well, what seems to be the problem with your car?"

"It won't start," she answered simply.

"Okay, let's take a look," Adam said as he led the way out to her car.

"What happened to laying down the law?" Lyndon asked just loud enough for Catherine to hear. She gave him an annoyed look and continued walking to her car. Adam wasted no time in popping the hood and began twiddling with every imaginable wire.

Catherine stood to the side and studied the mechanic as he looked at the under-hood contents. She noticed the long scar above his right eye. It looked as if he had had it for a while, and in a way it complimented his masculinity.

"Well, I can't tell what's wrong with it just from what I see here. I'll look it over and give you a call when I find the problem," Adam said as he closed the hood.

"How much will it cost for you to look it over?" Catherine tried to hide the insecurity from her voice.

"I'll tell you what," Adam began and motioned for them to follow him back to the office, "since you're Lyndon's friend, I won't charge you."

"Thank you, Mr. Carey. That's very kind."

"Don't mention it." Adam told her and held her with his gaze. Catherine didn't seem to mind. She was still trying to figure out how she knew this man. His face was unrecognizable, but something inside her felt drawn to him.

"I'll just have you fill out some information for the work order. Do you have your registration?" Adam asked when he was once again capable of thought.

"Yes. I left it in the car. I'll go get it."

Adam and Lyndon both stared after her as she left the office.

"That's some catch you've got there, Lyndon. She seems like a really nice girl."

"She's the most amazing woman I've ever met. She's smart, beautiful, hard-working, and her love for God is sincere."

"Wow! If I met a woman like that, I'd marry her before she could get away." Adam stopped just short of slapping Lyndon on the back, remembering his filthy hands.

Catherine re-entered the office and gave Adam the required information. Moments later, she and Lyndon were headed back to Star Lake.

"Was it just me, or did it seem like Carey was quite smitten with you?" Lyndon asked.

Catherine looked over at him in surprise.

"I think you imagined it. Are you jealous?"

"Should I be?"

It took a moment for Catherine to answer. How could she? There was something mysterious about Mr. Carey, and she wanted to know what.

"Whether or not you are jealous doesn't matter. We're not dating," she reminded him.

"You just say the word and we can be."

A sigh of relief escaped Catherine. She thought for sure that he would bring up the way she had acted with his arm around her in Carey's office. The proximity had been close and feelings had begun to cloud her judgment.

"So, do you feel better about the car situation?"

"Lyndon, I feel like I have to explain something. My brother died four years ago. He loved mechanical stuff, working on cars in his spare time. I just have a lot of memories surface when I'm in a place like that."

"I'm sorry that you lost your brother, Cat," Lyndon said sincerely.

"Thanks."

He still hadn't mentioned the way she'd looked at him in Carey's office by the time they had arrived back at Catherine's house and for that she was thankful.

"Should I pick you up in the morning?" Lyndon asked as he saw her to her door. The November air was chilly, so he didn't want to linger.

"Yes, please. Thanks for everything, Lyndon."

"You're welcome. I'll see you in the morning."

As Catherine watched him walk to his car, she was tempted to stop him, although she didn't know what for. Perhaps just to thank him for being patient.

Why do I feel like I know this woman? Adam asked himself as he looked down at the piece of paper Catherine had provided him with her first name and number at the office.

She was good about not giving out her personal information to people. After all, she was a young woman and it wasn't safe to give strangers access to her life.

Adam dialed the number and nervously ran his fingers over the piece of paper.

"Hello. This is Adam Carey. Is Catherine there?"

"Oh, hi, Adam. How are you?" Catherine said in a voice that was much too exuberant.

"I'm fine," he answered and found himself smiling at the sound of her voice. It was childish for a thirty-two year old to act this way, but involuntarily his smile remained in place.

"I've discovered the source of your car problems. Would you like me to tell you the options now, or do you have a way of getting here?"

"I'm borrowing my roommate's car so I can be there this afternoon if that's not too soon."

"It's perfect. I'll see you then."

Catherine sat staring at the phone long after she had said goodbye. She was driving to meet a man she'd only known for two days and she felt more elated than she ever had with Lyndon.

"I hardly recognized you," Catherine said as she stared at Adam Carey's clean clothes in amazement. The change it had produced was nothing short of remarkable. She was beginning to see how handsome he really was. She also realized how rude her comment had been.

"I'm sorry. That was inconsiderate of me," she apologized.

"Don't mention it. I quit early on Wednesdays so that I can make it to prayer meeting. Why don't you have a seat and we can discuss your car," Adam suggested as he pulled out a chair for her.

"You sound like a doctor."

"In a way I am. I have to know these machines inside out in order to treat the symptoms correctly."

"How long have you been a mechanic?"

"Oh, about ten years, I guess."

"Do you run this shop all by yourself?"

"Yes. I'm rather independent, so I like being self-employed."

"How long have you owned this shop?"

"You really are a journalist, aren't you?" Adam asked, trying to avoid her insistent inquiries.

"I'm sorry. Was I asking too many questions? I tend to do that when I meet new people," Catherine explained.

"I bet you're very good at your job," he said shyly.

"Lyndon seems to think so."

"He's a pretty cool guy. How long have you two been dating?" Adam asked out of curiosity.

"Oh, we're not dating. We're just good friends."

Adam nodded and thought back to the day he had met Catherine. He thought he had seen Lyndon's arm around her, but maybe there was an explanation. This certainly called for a conversation with Lyndon. If he gave him the right of way, Adam was sure to get to know this woman.

"So, what did you find on my car?"

"More things than I can list on one invoice," Adam answered truthfully and watched defeat rush over Catherine's face. "But all it needs to get it running is a starter."

"Are those expensive?"

"Not necessarily. I can get you a rebuilt one for a decent price."

"How long does it take to install? What's your hourly rate?"

Adam looked at her inquisitive face and once again felt something tug at his heart. Suddenly, he realized that the conversation with Lyndon was going to have to wait. He needed to spend time with this woman and find out what kind of spell she had cast over him.

"It's not that hard. It takes about as long as an oil change."

"I don't know a thing about cars. I can't even change a tire," Catherine admitted, not wanting to tell him that she was afraid of getting anywhere near the machines he worked with.

"Every woman should know how to change a tire. What if you got stranded in a snowstorm with a flat?"

"I guess I would just sit in the car and cry."

Adam laughed, revealing his perfect set of teeth and gorgeous smile.

"How about I put that starter in, and when you come to pick up your car, I'll teach you how to change a tire. Deal?"

"Deal," Catherine agreed without thinking.

And just how do you plan to explain this to Lyndon? She silently asked herself. *You can't even explain it to yourself.*

"I want to do a story."

Lyndon looked up from his computer to see Catherine standing in the doorway and greeted her with a warm smile. In a way, he was disappointed that Megan had let her borrow her car. He missed picking her up each morning and pretending that she needed him.

"What's wrong, Cat? Is the assignment you're working on not challenging enough?"

"That's not the problem. I think I've found something else I'd like to work on."

"Okay, I'm listening. What do you plan to do this story on?"

"Adam."

"Adam? Oh, you mean Carey."

Catherine nodded in confirmation.

"What could possibly be so interesting about him that you'd want to do a story about him?"

"That's not very nice, Lyndon," Catherine scolded him.

"You're right. I'm sorry." He paused for a moment. "You really think he's got a story locked up in his toolbox?"

"Of course. Why else would I have suggested it?"

Lyndon shrugged and gave her an incriminating grin.

"What?" Catherine asked insistently.

"I just wonder if you're making excuses to spend time with him."

"That's quite presumptuous, Lyndon. I'm going to forget you said that." She stared at him, but he just stared back, looking unshakable.

"Lyndon, let's not fight about this. Do I have your permission to do a story on Adam and his shop, or am I going to have to do it on my own time?"

"You have my permission," Lyndon said in defeat.

"Why, thank you, Mr. Reinhardt. I won't let you down."

She turned and left his office, stifling the urge to do a cartwheel across the floor out of sheer joy. This was sure to be her best story yet.

Adam smiled as Catherine, looking rather professional in her black pants and sweater, walked through the door. She had her long, blonde hair pulled back in a way that made her look younger than he assumed her to be.

"Hello, Adam," she greeted him.

"Tell me, Catherine, have you ever heard the phrase 'dress for the occasion'?"

"Yes, I have, but unlike you, I have to look spiffy for work."

"Spiffy, huh? Well, you certainly can't change a tire in those clothes," Adam told her as he stepped around the corner into what looked like a hallway. Catherine heard a locker open and close. Adam reappeared seconds later with a pair of blue coveralls pinned beneath his arm and an adorable grin on his jagged face.

"They're going to be baggy, but they'll save that nice outfit," he explained and handed the coveralls to her. "The bathroom's right through there if you think you need some privacy."

Catherine thanked him and made her way across the room and through the doorway he had just entered. Adam leaned against his invoice-covered desk and stared at the floor. He knew he was in dangerous territory. If Lyndon had feelings for this woman, it was wrong of him to intrude. Yet, as much as he truly believed that, he still found himself hoping that her car would require maintenance again very soon.

"I'm ready."

Adam snapped from his thoughts to find Catherine looking down intently at the sleeves she was attempting to roll up. The coveralls hung loosely over her body and did nothing for her figure.

"Do you need some help?"

She gave him an inept look and nodded.

"Rolling your sleeves up with one hand is harder than it looks," Catherine admitted as she held one arm out to him. He gently maneuvered the sleeves with his fingers until they fit snugly above her elbows on both arms.

"There. Now you look ready to work."

"I don't understand," Catherine began as they made their way into the repair bay. "You said that you would teach me how to change a tire. You didn't say anything about working."

"I have a firm theory about learning. You will never learn anything by watching someone else do it," Adam said as he pointed to a jack lying against the wall. "Roll the jack over here and line it up with the frame. Make sure this knob is tight so you're not losing air pressure. Once it's lined up, just start pumping the handle."

He watched as Catherine followed his directions.

"Adam?" she began as she worked with the jack. "Whose car is this?"

"It doesn't matter. They would immediately agree when they found out that you had never done this before. They would definitely want you to learn."

Catherine nodded and pointed to the jack.

"Is that high enough?"

"Yep."

"Now what do I do?"

Adam smiled and walked across the bay.

"Most people with a flat tire on the side of the road don't have this luxury," he said as he brought out a rolling seat and set it down in front of the tire, "but I'm going to give you the special treatment."

Catherine thanked him and took a seat. Adam handed her a large, four-sided, pipe-looking tool.

"This is a tire iron. See how it has four sides? Just find the one that fits on the lug-nut and fit it over it."

"Like this?"

"Good. Now turn it to the left as hard as you can."

Catherine gripped the wrench with both hands and pushed with all her might, but the nut made no sign of movement. She released her hands, repositioned them and tried again, but still the nut remained motionless. She looked helplessly up at Adam and found him trying to hide his smile.

"Now what do I do?" Catherine asked cynically.

"Now you let me help you."

Adam knelt down beside her and placed his hands along side of hers on the wrench. Catherine began to feel dizzy, which she attributed to a lack of oxygen; she hadn't taken a breath since Adam had come close to her.

"Ready?"

Catherine nodded.

"One, two, three."

The nuts were removed in no time at all. Catherine was amazed--not only at her unexplainable attraction to this man, but also by the equally astounding strength he possessed.

"What would I do if I were alone and couldn't get those loose?"

"I guess you'd have to sit in your car and cry."

Catherine graced him with a laugh and he had no choice but to ask her the question that had been constantly weighing on his mind.

"I keep getting the feeling that we've known each other for a long time. Do you get that impression, too?"

"I do, but I don't know why," Catherine admitted. She felt a connection to Adam that she couldn't explain. He was so different from Lyndon. With Lyndon, she always felt as if she was trying too hard to care for him the same way he did for her. With Adam, she had to make a conscious effort not to throw her arms around him.

Adam reached in front of her and began gathering the lug nuts in his hands. Catherine studied his profile and once again admired the scar on his forehead. It seemed to suit him so entirely that she couldn't imagine him without it.

"How did you get that scar?" she asked, hoping it wasn't too personal of a question.

"In an accident."

Catherine could see that he had no intention of elaborating on the subject so she steered the conversation back to the task at hand.

"What's next?"

"Take hold of the tire on both sides and pull it toward you. Make sure to watch your feet."

In one swift motion, Catherine removed the tire and smiled with pride at Adam.

"Good. Now put it back on."

Catherine frowned and Adam waved a finger at her.

"I don't tolerate complaining in my classroom."

"I'm sorry," she said and proceeded to struggle with the tire. After a couple of tries, she succeeded. When all of the lug nuts were replaced and finger tight, Adam handed her another tool she'd never seen before.

"Here's another luxury you won't have. It's called a torque wrench. Put it on the nut and turn it to the right until you feel it break."

"It's going to break?" Catherine asked anxiously.

"No, no. Not like that. I'm sorry," Adam apologized. He had never dealt one-on-one with someone with such elementary mechanical skills. He liked it, though. It gave him a protective feeling to know that it was he who was teaching this special woman.

"Just stop when you feel it give way," he explained and watched as she nodded her head in understanding. Not long after that, she was dusting off her hands and waiting for Adam's approval.

"You're a fast learner."

"Thank you, but I still have a question. If I don't have a torque wrench with me, how do I know how much to tighten the nuts?"

"Just tighten them as much as you can, and then take your car to a qualified mechanic as soon as possible. They'll torque it down, but most of the time you'll just be using a spare. It's fine to just tighten them down with the tire iron."

Adam then showed her how to let the jack down. After the tools were put away, they made their way back into the office.

"Would you like a cup of coffee?"

"No, thank you, but water would be nice. Do you mind if I stay a few minutes? There is something I would like to discuss with you."

"All right. I'll get us something to drink. Feel free to get out of those coveralls," Adam said, making his way to the faucet to fill the coffee pot.

Five minutes later, they sat down across from each other. Adam was enjoying the warmth of his cup of coffee and wondering why Catherine had settled for just water. She was once again in her own clothes instead of Adam's coveralls and sat quietly across the desk.

"So, what do you want to talk about?"

"I would like to write a story about you."

Adam set his mug on the desk and leaned forward. His brow was lowered in perplexity, making his scar stand out.

"A story on me? I didn't know you wrote fictitious stories, Catherine."

"I don't."

"Then what's so exceptional about me?"

"That's what I'd like to find out. I'm not a naturally nosey person, Adam, but there's something mysterious about you, and I want to know what it is."

"Mysterious, huh?" Adam ran his fingers over his bristly chin in contemplation. He honestly didn't know why she would have an interest in his life, but if it allowed him to spend more time with her, then he was all for it.

"If this is something you really want to do, I would be a fool to stand in your way. When would you like to begin the interrogation?"

Catherine gave him a smile that spoke volumes. She truly was trying not to give away the involuntary attraction she was feeling, but its power overrode her efforts to conceal it.

"What time is best for you? I mean, you are the busy one," Catherine chided him.

"How about Saturday? You can meet me here and begin the quiz."

"Sounds good to me."

"Good. Now tell me--do you feel confident about your tire-changing experience? Do you think you'd be able to do it in a pinch?"

"Of course. Especially if you're there helping me." Catherine suddenly realized that she was flirting. It was something she wasn't accustomed to and it surprised her. She placed her empty glass on the desk and grabbed her purse.

"I really appreciate you helping me out, Adam. How much do I owe you?" She opened her checkbook and took a pen from his desk. Adam scribbled the price on an invoice and handed it to her. She filled out her check for the proper amount and placed it in his work-worn hand. Adam, out of habit, glanced at the top left corner of her check.

Catherine Scott.

He studied her name intently, and his mind began to swarm with ideas, as if he had been staring at the puzzle pieces for so long and finally caught a glimpse of the photo on the box. It was all coming together so quickly. He suddenly realized why she looked and seemed so familiar.

"I'll call you tomorrow so that we can coordinate our plans for Saturday." Adam stood and held out his hand to her.

"Thanks for everything, Adam," Catherine said as she stood and returned his handshake.

Adam smiled and shook his head.

"You know, you're one of the few that don't call me Carey."

"Does that bother you?"

"No, not at all. You can call me anything you'd like."

They shared a smile, both knowing that something remarkable was happening before their very eyes.

"I'll see you Saturday, Catherine."

"Please, feel free to call me Katie."

Katie!

With one word she banished all of Adam's hopes. He now knew exactly who she was. She was Katie Scott, and she would never let him into her life.

"Is there something on your mind, Katie? You seem kind of distant," Evan Scott inquired of his oldest daughter. He had called just to touch base with her. It was something that he made a point to do as often as possible.

"I have been thinking about how my life for the past four years has been somewhat uneventful. Now, suddenly it seems as if my world has been turned upside down with all kinds of stuff."

"I'm sorry to hear that you feel so out of control. Is there anything I can do to help?"

"I'm afraid not, Dad."

"Well, we'll pray for you," Evan assured her. "We're looking forward to spending Thanksgiving with you next week. Your mother wanted me to tell you to bring along your *friend.*" Catherine couldn't miss his emphasis.

"You mean Lyndon, my *boss.*"

"Sure. Bring him, too."

"Okay, Dad. I'll see you next week," Catherine bid him goodbye and placed her cordless phone on the kitchen counter.

Only one hour remained before she was to meet Adam. She stared at the counter and thought back on her conversation with Lyndon on Wednesday evening.

"An interview with Carey at his shop? I must say, I'm a little concerned, Cat."

"Why? I've interviewed many individuals alone. Besides, you said yourself that he was trustworthy."

"Oh, don't turn this around to make me the enemy. I'm beginning to wonder if introducing the two of you was a mistake."

Catherine didn't blame him for his hostility. In his shoes, she'd feel the same. That was one of the reasons it had been so hard to inform him of her appointment with Adam. She had told Lyndon that this was a work-related engagement only, but she couldn't keep from hoping that it would turn out to be something more.

A noise from the front door caught her attention.

"You're home early. That must mean job hunting either went really well, or didn't go at all."

Megan set her keys on the counter and smiled at Catherine.

"So, you found a job?"

"Yes."

"That's great. Tell me everything."

"The insurance agency in town needed someone to sort through files and answer the phone. Typing was the only prerequisite."

"You've become a secretary," Catherine stated.

She and Megan were back on good terms. At first, Megan couldn't stand that the very man who had fired her was someone Catherine called a friend, but over time she accepted it and moved on. Catherine rarely ever saw her due to the fact that she spent most of her days and nights with Tim, her official boyfriend.

"They don't call it a secretary. It's a litigation specialist. Anyway, I can start on Monday. The pay is decent and I get benefits. Maybe getting fired will be the best thing that's ever happened to me."

Catherine smiled at her friend's enthusiasm, but she didn't share it. When she looked back on the incident, she was still amazed that Lyndon had done such a cold and heartless thing as firing Megan. Since that day, he had shown no sign of that type of behavior, but she was sure that if provoked, he could revert back to the old Lyndon.

"What about you? How was your day?"

"Wonderful," Catherine answered, her face dreamy.

"Oh, no. You've got that look."

"What look?"

"I don't know how to explain it. You just have that look. Obviously, something remarkable happened."

"Remarkable, extravagant--I don't know a word that could define Adam. I just know that he's unlike any man I've ever met."

"Whoa, hold up. Who's this guy?"

"He's the mechanic who fixed my car."

"Are you sure that's all he did?" Megan asked sarcastically.

Catherine ignored her and went on.

"He's kind of quiet, but he has a great sense of humor. He runs the whole business by himself and still makes time for church, even on Wednesday night. I feel so strange when I'm around him, but in a good way. We talk and laugh like we've known each other for years. You know how people say that when you meet the right one, you'll know? I don't want to jump to conclusions, but I think that's the feeling I get when I'm with Adam. It's more than attraction; it's like we were destined to know each other in one way or another."

"I don't think you're jumping to conclusions, Katie. I just think you're crazy. What does Lyndon have to say about this?" Megan was curious to know if he had lost his sanity upon finding out that his most prized employee no longer needed him.

"I didn't elaborate on the bond that Adam and I seem to share, but I did ask if I could write a story about him. Lyndon agreed, as did Adam. I'm interviewing him tonight."

Megan shook her head.

"I think you're getting in way over your head. Take my word for it: juggling two men at once is never a good idea."

Catherine couldn't agree more. It was a risky race she was in. Her problem was that she didn't know which man to drop out of the running. The ringing of the phone startled her from her perturbed state of mind.

"Is this Catherine?"

"Hi, Lyndon. How are you?"

Megan took that as her cue and drifted off down the hall to her room.

"I'd be better if you were going out with me tonight instead of Carey."

"Is that all you called about?"

"No. I wanted to say hi."

"That was nice of you. While I have you on the phone, I'd like to invite you to Thanksgiving dinner at my parents' home. I'm just going for the day. Would you like to come?"

"I'd love to. What can I bring?"

"Just yourself."

"All right. I guess I'll see you on Sunday, then," Lyndon said in closing. He could tell by her tone that she wanted to get going.

"Yep. I'll see you then."

Catherine felt guilty for practically pushing him off the other line, but she didn't want to be late. She couldn't be.

The first thing that caught Catherine's attention was the clean-shaven man with sandy hair who was waiting to greet her. All she could do was stare until Adam rescued her by offering to take her jacket.

"I don't think I've ever seen you this..." Catherine searched in vain for the right words to describe his clean-cut appearance.

"Spiffy?" Adam offered.

Catherine laughed at the way he read her mind. Adam took in the genuine look of delight in her eyes and prayed that his eyes didn't give away his heart as hers did.

Why do you have to be who you are, Katie? Why, even after discovering our uncanny connection, do I smile when I think of you?

After taking a seat, Catherine retrieved her notebook from her purse. Opening it to a blank page, she set it in front of her.

"Why do I feel like you're conducting an experiment on me?" Adam asked.

Catherine shrugged and asked the first of many questions.

"Do you live here in town?"

"Yes."

"Alone?"

"Are all the questions going to be this personal?"

"If I'm going to write a story, it's going to be personal. Therefore, some of the questions must be as well."

Adam nodded and sipped his coffee while Catherine continued.

"What made you decide to live here?"

"My uncle owned this shop. I came here right out of college to work with him. When he passed away, he left it to me. I've been here ever since."

"How old are you, Adam?"

"Is that really necessary?"

"Yes."

"I'm thirty-two."

"Wow," Catherine said without thinking.

"You think I'm old? How old are you?"

"I'm not the one being interviewed." Adam laughed at her quick answer, and a series of questions followed, including ones about his family and his career. Adam answered every question promptly and honestly until Catherine inquired about the accident that had produced the noticeable scar that he bore.

"That's the one question I won't answer."

Catherine nodded, but displayed a look of pure disappointment. It was obvious to her that Adam had a secret and therein was her story. She would never get anywhere if he didn't open up to her. It seemed that she had his trust but was it really possible to trust someone you had just met?

Adam watched her closely and could see that his secretive behavior was bothering her. He hated holding back the answers she so desperately wanted, but he knew that he had no other option. She would hate him if she knew the truth.

I want to tell you, Katie, and I will someday.

"You're not mad at me, are you?" he asked.

"No. When I'm mad, you'll know." Catherine narrowed her eyes and tightly pressed her lips together. Adam gave her a smile and she returned one of her own, leaving Adam amazed at how much she looked like her brother when she smiled. Jesse Scott had had the same childish sparkle.

Adam forced himself back to the present. If he didn't think clearly, he was going to give himself away.

They talked for half an hour more before parting. Adam was grateful for the silent ride home. He spent it in serious consideration and prayer.

"Well, is he a keeper?" Megan asked as soon as Catherine opened the front door later that evening.

"I certainly hope so. It would be awfully difficult to throw him back." She took a seat on the couch.

"I take it everything went well."

"Indeed." Catherine's eyes were dreamy as she spoke and Megan laughed at her.

"You are quite smitten, I'd say."

"So would I."

"When are you going to tell Lyndon?"

"We're going to my parents' for Thanksgiving dinner. I'll tell him after that. I'm going to need some time to find the right words."

"Good luck," Megan said as she turned the TV back on. "You'll need it."

Lyndon took a deep breath and slowly released it. Never before had he felt so ill at ease. Catherine had offered to drive for the duration of the trip, and now he was thankful that he had agreed.

"Are you all right?"

He looked over at her. From his view in the passenger seat, she looked as beautifully calm as ever. He tried to smile at her, but the effort only magnified his insecurity.

"Are you nervous?" Catherine asked her companion. This was a first for her as well. It was all new and frightening, especially due to the fact that she had no interest in him. In a way, she felt sorry for him. He had the potential to be a wonderful husband to someone; just not her. What he needed was a woman who loved him enough to overlook his demanding, sometimes childish, behavior. Catherine was sure that she could not be that woman.

"There's nothing to worry about, Lyndon," she tried to assure him. "You've already met my mom and Leah. All you have to endure is meeting my dad."

"Does he think we're dating?"

"No. If he did, then you'd really have a reason to worry."

"Why's that? Has he inflicted some kind of bodily harm on the other men you've brought home?"

"No." Catherine didn't bother telling him that he was the only man she'd ever brought home. "My dad's just a little protective of his older daughter, that's all."

Lyndon nodded and took in the large farmhouse that was just coming into view.

"Here it is."

The anxiety rose within him. He made an attempt to calm the butterflies that were executing head-spinning maneuvers in his stomach. However, his fears dissipated the moment he shook Evan Scott's hand. Catherine had been right; there was nothing to fret over. Although Evan didn't look a thing like his daughter, Lyndon could see a strong resemblance in their soft expressions and behavior.

The women went to work on the meal while Lyndon and Evan, thankful that their gender rarely took part in this annual meal preparation, made their way into the living room to get better acquainted.

"So, Katie tells me that you're her boss," Evan began. "I assume she means at work."

Lyndon could see where Catherine's sense of humor came from.

"Yes, at work. But most of my employees would tell you that's debatable."

"It must be difficult to have that kind of responsibility at your age."

"It certainly is. Catherine for the most part has no confidence in my leadership abilities," Lyndon confessed and stared toward the kitchen where the woman he spoke of worked busily with her mother and sister.

"Katie's unique like that," Evan explained. "She'll politely keep her opinion to herself until you ask for it. Then watch out because she'll make no attempt to conceal it."

"You've got that right."

"Leah's just the opposite. She'll blurt out the most unexpected idea without warning. You never can tell what's going to come out of her mouth."

Lyndon smiled and remembered some of the unruly comments Leah had made the day he had met her.

The conversation turned to Lyndon's background, and Evan listened intently as the younger man spoke. Neither man would have been so relaxed had they been able to hear the discussion in the next room.

Chapter Seven

"Should I butter these rolls?" Leah asked as she brought the tray from the oven.

"Sure, honey," Robin answered and then turned her attention to her older daughter.

"How's your car running now, Katie?"

"It runs as rickety as ever, but it starts like a champ. The best part is that it didn't cost me an arm and a leg."

"Aren't you glad Lyndon suggested that repair shop?"

"Yeah," Catherine answered absently. She had unknowingly ceased her stirring of the gravy and was now staring blankly at the stove. Her mother had read the thoughts of her mind flawlessly. She was indeed very thankful that Lyndon had recommended Adam. She somehow knew that in one way or another, he would transform her life.

"It would make things so much easier for us--not to mention Lyndon--if you'd stop denying and just admit it," Leah interjected, snapping Catherine from her daydream and causing her to resume the task of stirring the now bubbling gravy.

"Admit what?"

"Katie, it's obvious that you're in love," Robin said softly.

"I definitely have an infatuation, Mom, but not with the man sitting in our living room."

Robin stopped just short of dropping the dish of mashed potatoes she was holding. She spun around and stared speechless at Catherine. Her eyes were wide in disbelief. Leah's face was expressionless, although she was equally dumbfounded. She was trying to decide if she had or had not just imagined her sister's words.

"I know it sounds crazy," Catherine began helplessly. "Actually, I know it's crazy. I shouldn't feel this way but I can't seem to help it."

"Who are you talking about, Catherine?" Robin questioned.

"His name is Adam. He's the mechanic who fixed my car."

"You've known him for a matter of weeks and you're in love with him?"

"I didn't say that," Catherine answered in defense. Her voice was hushed to prevent it from traveling beyond the room. "I understand your caution, Mom. I have no explanation for these feeling or an excuse for not caring for Lyndon."

"Does he know you like this other guy?" Leah spoke for the first time since Catherine's declaration.

"I'm going to tell him on our way home. It's not fair to let him believe that we have a future, regardless of what happens with Adam."

All three women were momentarily silent. Leah's face looked sullen, due to the pity she felt for Lyndon. Sure, he had his faults, but overall he was a nice man.

Robin was still in shock. Catherine had spoken of a crush from time to time in years past, but never had she reacted like this. This was so unlike anything she'd ever done. She was always so sensible and collected. It was strange to see her so bothered.

"Leah, please go tell your father and Lyndon that we're ready."

After hesitating for just a fraction of a second, Leah left the kitchen to do as she was told.

"Katie, is this other man a Christian?" Robin asked gently as she placed her hands on Catherine's shoulders and looked her squarely in the eye.

"Yes. Adam takes his walk with God very seriously."

"All right, then. For the time being, I have no objections. Be smart, though. It's not like you to be so enraptured. Is it okay if I tell your father about this?"

"Sure, Mom."

"My only request is that you tell Lyndon as soon as possible that you are not interested."

"I will."

Later, as the Scott family and their guest bowed their heads to say thanks for the food and their abundance of blessings, Catherine silently prayed that she would have the right words to tell Lyndon that her heart was residing elsewhere.

A light snow was falling as Evan Scott walked toward the house. He had made his nightly check on the animals and was ready to call it a day. The kitchen was dark as he stepped inside, except for the light above the stove. When he reached for the switch, he saw a figure in the doorway. He turned and smiled as Robin walked toward him. The couple shared a long embrace in the silent stillness of the room.

"It was a good day, wasn't it?" Evan asked, his arms still around his wife.

"Yes. Did I mention how thankful I am for you?"

"No, but you can show me."

Robin smiled and kissed him gently.

"I love you, Evan."

"I love you," he answered and pulled her close. Husband and wife stared out the window at the falling snow, marveling at its gracefulness and soaking up the beauty of the night.

"Speaking of love," Evan began. "What exactly is going on between Katie and Lyndon?"

"I think it's what's *not* going on that is the bigger concern."

"What do you mean by that? He seemed quite enthralled with her."

"Oh, he is, but she's preoccupied with someone else."

"Who?"

"The mechanic."

"The shy one she spoke of?"

"Yes. I've never seen Katie act the way she did today. I guess we'll just have to wait and see what becomes of this."

"Well, one thing is for sure," Evan said as he turned off the stove light. "I admire any man who's not afraid to get his hands dirty."

"As do I," Robin said as she took his hand and led him from the room.

"You may look like your mother, but you have your father's personality," Lyndon said as soon as they were on the road. The day, in his opinion, had gone very well. They had shared a wonderful meal and had relaxed for the rest of the afternoon.

"Dad and I are very much alike," Catherine said, hoping that he had not caught her nervous tone.

"Are you okay? You were kind of quiet all afternoon." He looked over at her in the dark and tried to read the expression on her face. She looked thoughtful as she stared through the windshield.

"I'm fine. I just have a lot on my mind."

"Me, too," Lyndon carefully weighed out his next words. "Cat, I had such a great time today. It seems like forever since we've spent time together. It was nice just to be near you all day. I know that I don't own you, but it seems that you're spending time with Carey and not enough with me."

Catherine knew the time was now. She had to tell him. Besides, he had brought up the subject and if she didn't do it now, she may never at all.

"We need to talk, Lyndon," she began and glanced over at him to ensure that she had his attention. "First, I need to reiterate that our relationship doesn't go beyond friendship. Secondly, I need to know if we will still be friends if I ever decide to date someone else." She thought it best not to mention any names in case nothing became of her feelings for Adam.

For a whole minute Lyndon was silent, leaving Catherine helpless in dealing with the uncomfortable tension.

"I don't understand, Cat. I thought you were beginning to like me." His voice was so hurt that for a moment Catherine considered taking back her words.

"I do care, Lyndon. I just don't have the same feelings you do."

Lyndon didn't bother asking who it was when she mentioned dating someone else. He had seen it that first day in Carey's small office. The way they had looked at each other had been engraved in his mind. The thought of her with anyone caused anger to rise within him. How could she just turn away from him like this? Especially after she had seemed to have changed the way she viewed him. He'd let his guard down, and she'd taken his heart. Now he kicked himself for being so careless.

The ironic part was that he was the one to blame. In his desire to look after her, he had introduced her to the man who had apparently claimed her heart.

"I hope this doesn't affect our friendship or our working relationship," Catherine muttered toward his silence.

"Are you kidding? This changes everything! I can't believe you're telling me this."

Catherine had no idea how to respond to his anger-filled outburst, so she remained silent. In fact, they both refused to speak until they arrived at Lyndon's apartment. Although Catherine had assumed that he would climb from the car without hesitation, he shocked her when he didn't so much as reach for the door handle. There was no movement, no sound, only the rickety hum of the engine. He finally turned and looked at her.

"Catherine, please reconsider." He reached to touch her face, but stopped when he remembered her warning from the day he had kissed her in the office. "Don't you see that I can give you everything you need?"

"Lyndon," she began, but found no appropriate words to follow with. "I'm sorry."

Lyndon turned back to the front and took a deep breath in attempt to regain control of his emotions.

"Well, if I can't make you happy, then I hope *he* does."

With that he left the car, quickly making his way to his apartment, without looking back. Once inside, he leaned against the door and closed his eyes.

I don't understand, Lord. I thought she was the one. I feel that I love her, but is it love if she doesn't love me back? Help me to know what to do.

"Carey's Automotive."

"Hi, Adam. This is Catherine."

"Let, me guess: you thought of some more questions for me."

"Yes, I did," Catherine said as she leaned back in her office chair. It had taken some time to come up with a way to talk to him again, but she figured her story was the best excuse she had. "You told me that you came to work for your uncle right after college. What did you go to college for?"

"Missions. I completed my degree thinking that I would set off on deputation and then the mission field, but I guess the Lord had other plans. Now I believe any place can be a mission field. Just because I can't go to a foreign country to spread the gospel, doesn't mean I can't support someone who does."

"So, your uncle needed help and you considered it just as much of a calling as missions?"

"Yes."

"Would you still like to be a missionary someday?"

"If God provides the opportunity, I would."

"Not many people would let go of their dream without a fight, like you did," Catherine commended him.

"I've learned that God's plan is bigger than mine."

Catherine couldn't help but respect Adam for the earnest way he sought after Christ-likeness. The indescribable feeling within her was becoming more and more overwhelming with each passing day. She wished it was possible to sit and talk to Adam all day, but she knew that they both had work to do.

"Thanks for your time, Adam."

"No problem. If you think of any more questions, just give me a call."

"I will."

Although Catherine bid him goodbye, her thoughts were still wrapped around him.

This article isn't going to write itself, Catherine. Stop staring at the computer screen and type something.

Catherine placed her hands on the keyboard, but her fingers remained motionless. Lyndon had allowed her three days to create the article she was currently working on and now it was due on the copy editor's desk in a matter of hours. Unfortunately, she had yet to write one word of it.

Procrastination was something she had never allowed in her life. To her, it was as wrong as impulsiveness. For some reason, she was now seeing signs of both on a daily basis.

How can I focus on this story when my mind is constantly being diverted back to a certain mechanic with blue eyes? Did I so completely confuse Adam's kindness with interest? I've never felt a connection like this in such a short amount of time. Was I just imagining that he felt it, too?

Impatiently, she began rhythmically tapping her pen against her notebook. Life had been so placid before she had met Adam. Even her situation with Lyndon, given some time, would have worked itself out. In this case, she was helpless, inept, and unable to think of anything but Adam Carey every moment of her day. It was unbiblical and unhealthy.

Lord, please help me to focus on You. No man should occupy this much space in my mind.

Catherine nearly jumped from her skin when her phone rang. She cleared her throat and answered.

"Journalism department. Catherine Scott."

"Hi, Cat."

"Lyndon? Where are you?"

"In my office."

Catherine turned in her chair and looked across the room. There he was, seated royally in his leather chair with the phone cradled between his ear and shoulder. His dark eyes smiled playfully at her, causing her to turn and face her computer.

"Are you really so lazy that you can't walk forty feet to say hello?"

"Didn't you once tell me that I should be more discreet?"

"Yes."

"Well, that's what I'm doing. You look like you need some help," Lyndon commented.

"Are you spying on me?"

"Yes."

Catherine laughed and looked at her blank computer screen. It seemed that Lyndon was once again comfortable with their friendship. For that she was grateful. Or was he too stubborn to give up his relentless pursuit?

"I just can't seem to concentrate. This is due in two hours. I don't suppose I can get another day, can I?"

"Nope. I can't play favorites. Remember?"

"Was there any specific reason you called?" Catherine asked insistently.

"No. Just let me know if you need my help."

When she hung up, Catherine couldn't resist looking over her shoulder. As if he had been waiting for her to turn around, Lyndon winked at her and then went back to his typing.

By some miracle, the copy editor had Catherine's article on his desk before the deadline. Where the words came from, she did not know. Perhaps Megan had passed on her gift of extemporaneous writing to her best friend when she left. If so, Catherine would be sure to thank her.

It was unusual for Adam to stay behind at the shop any longer than needed, but tonight he made an exception. The day had dragged by in slow motion. His job was one that demanded constant concentration for both efficiency and safety, but he had found himself daydreaming on more than one occasion.

Attraction was nothing new to him. At thirty-two he had felt it more times than he could remember. This was different. It was as different as it was strange and unfamiliar. If Catherine had been anyone else, he had a strong suspicion that by now he would be considering spending the rest of his life with her. Unfortunately, it wasn't an option because of the simple fact that she was Jesse Scott's sister.

It hurt him terribly to be so deceitful to a woman who obviously was seeking something he could not give her. Love, respect, companionship, and laughter he could and would gladly give in a moment's notice. But all these characteristics, noble as they may be, could never compensate for the omission of honesty.

I know you must be confused, Katie. I am, too. You must be wondering why I'm distant, but I promise you that I have no choice. If I allow myself to be near you, I'm quite sure I'd fall for you. I'm so sorry Jesse's not here. If I had just been stronger..."

Adam shook his head at his thoughts. There was no practicality in wishful thinking. He had spent the past four years blaming himself. The only thing it had produced was a waste of time. He was sure that he'd never forget the accident, but every day brought him one step closer to forgiving himself for it.

Armed with only motivation, Catherine marched into Lyndon's office and slapped the note on his desk. The look on her face as she took a seat and crossed her legs told him she was ready for battle.

"What is that supposed to mean?" she asked and pointed to the note.

Lyndon shrugged. "It means just what it says; I wanted to see you in my office right away."

"Okay, I'm here. What's the reason behind your urgency?" Catherine hated sounding so short, but involuntarily every word out of her mouth sounded annoyed and impatient.

Lyndon stood, smoothed his tie and walked toward the door. After closing it gently he leaned against it and crossed his arms. It took a while for Catherine to realize he wasn't coming back to his desk. She pivoted in her chair and stared at him.

"What's going on?" she asked.

"Let's put our feelings, or lack of, aside for a moment," he suggested as he made his way across the room and stood beside her. "Right now I'm Mr. Reinhardt and you're Miss Scott."

"Am I getting fired? Did I do something wrong?"

"No. I just want to know what's troubling you. I'd be blind if I didn't notice how slack your work is becoming. I asked you here because, as your boss, I care about you."

Catherine took a long moment to try and cool down. Lyndon's concern touched her. "It's just…" she began and slapped the arm of the chair with her palm, stood, and walked to the window. "I feel so irritable. It's nothing that you, or anyone here, have done."

"Then what is it?"

"It's the thing with Adam."

The words were out of her mouth before she knew she had said them.

"What thing with Adam?"

"The story, of course," Catherine answered in a tone that was half truthful.

"What about a story could possibly make you so perturbed?" Lyndon asked. His exterior was calm, but he was suffocating under his anger. "Cat, tell me the truth."

Catherine felt so ashamed. How could she admit her feelings about Adam to a man who had his own feelings for her? It was inconsiderate, to say the least.

"Lyndon, I don't think you'll want to hear what I have to say."

"Tell me, Cat." His voice was demanding and Catherine turned toward the window to avoid him.

"Lyndon, you don't--"

"Tell me."

"Fine. But, I'm telling you as your employee. Please, remember that." Catherine took a deep breath and began. "I thought we had something, Adam and I. I felt a connection and I thought he felt it too."

"So, what happened?"

"Nothing. That's what's bothering me. At first, he seemed interested, but now it's like he's afraid of something."

Lyndon closed his eyes in an attempt to block out the image of her with anyone other than him. Carey was a good man, and Lyndon respected him, but it made no difference. The thought of Catherine giving her love to anyone else made him boil with rage.

When he opened his eyes, all bitterness fled from his body. He stared at Catherine gazing out the window. There was no doubt in his mind that she was the very essence of everything beautiful. He walked slowly over to the window and stood beside her. The sweet smell of her perfume mesmerized him, and for several moments all he could do was gawk at her. Unconsciously, he reached out and gently placed his hand on her arm. He assumed she would be startled by his touch, but instead, she was still as if she had expected it.

"Why, Lyndon?"

"Why what?" he asked as he studied her long blonde hair, wondering if it felt as soft as it looked.

"Why do you care so much when I offer you nothing in return?" *Here I stand pouring out my heart about Adam, knowing how you feel about me, and you don't say a thing. You just listen.*

"I'm a very patient man."

"No, you're not," Catherine clarified with a laugh and turned to him. Her smile faded when she saw the intent look in his dark gray eyes. She studied him, trying to gauge his next move. Lyndon moved his eyes from hers and found himself hypnotized by her lips. He wanted so badly to kiss her again, but knew that he was uninvited. Instead, he gently brushed her face with the back of his hand.

"I'm right here, waiting," he said, his voice warm. She nodded her head in understanding and prayed that he couldn't see the pounding in her chest that his touch had induced.

Lyndon forced himself to turn and sit down at his desk.

"Just hang in there, Catherine. Everything will turn out all right."

"Thanks," she replied and made her way to the door but turned before opening it.

"You're not angry with me are you, Lyndon?"

"Never."

Catherine smiled at her boss and then was gone. The sound of the door closing was like an omen to him. It was as if she had done the same to their relationship. It would seem like that which had never begun, had ended.

"What about this one?"

"No. It's too girly," Catherine answered, rejecting the pink blouse Megan was holding. "Remember, this is Leah we're shopping for."

"Oh, yeah. I forgot."

Catherine smiled and went back to rifling through the rack of clothes. The perfect gift could be directly under her nose, and she wouldn't see it. Her feet may have been planted on the shiny department store floor, but her mind was miles away--five miles, actually. Going shopping had been her idea, but Megan had insisted on choosing the location. Catherine calmly agreed and even acted normally as they had entered the town in which Adam Carey lived.

The stores, the signs, the people, and even the cars all reminded her of Adam. Driving through the town, she had focused intently on the road ahead. If not, she would have crashed while attempting to spot him among the many passersby.

Now, she stood in the store pretending to look at clothes. In the past week, she had been doing very well, holding her thoughts of Adam Carey at bay. But, being in this town today, it was as if he were just over her shoulder, watching her every move. It gave her an uneasy, wonderful feeling.

With a graceful tilt of her head, she closed her eyes and tried to recapture the feeling of Adam's nearness. His strong hands had been nothing but gentle as he had helped her roll up her sleeves that day in his office. She liked the way he smelled of musk, sweat, and brake fluid. She was tempted to intentionally break something on her car, just so she could watch his face light up with pride when he had fixed it.

"Katie?"

Catherine opened up her eyes to find Megan impatiently holding up another shirt for her inspection.

"Oh, that's perfect. Where did you find it?"

"It's the same one I just showed you," Megan declared, tossing the shirt back on the rack. "What is going on with you? You've been like this since we got here. And since when do you wait until the week before Christmas to buy your presents?"

"I'm just distracted."

"Oh, no. Which one is it this time? The overbearing, offer-you-everything boss, or the mysterious, irresistible mechanic?"

"The blue-eyed, needs-a-shave mechanic. I haven't heard from him since Thanksgiving, and I'm wondering if maybe it's time to set up another interview. He works here in town." She threw in the last part for emphasis.

"Would you like to visit him while we're here? I'd certainly like to meet the subject of so many of our conversations." Megan's tone was sarcastic.

"Thanks, but no thanks. I rather enjoy breathing and it's something I'm apt not to do when I'm around him."

"Okay, suit yourself," Megan said as she shuffled toward the intimate section of the lady's department to do a little shopping for herself. Catherine followed and they spent the next five minutes laughing at the various skimpy arrangements. A swath of leopard-skin fabric caught Catherine's attention, and she held the flashy bra by the hanger, letting it dangle in front of her.

"Meg, wait until you see this one…"

The grin on Catherine's face vanished when she turned around and met the wide eyes of Adam Carey, who was passing by in a nearby aisle. With her mouth open in disbelief she followed his gaze to the article she held in front of her. Turning, she quickly hung it on the nearest rack and told herself not to faint. Never before had her face felt so hot.

When she turned back to Adam, she could see his lips were tight in an attempt to conceal a smile. Catherine tried to say something, but her words tripped over each other. Speechless, she stared at Adam's attractive but gruff face and the blue eyes that laughed at her. She tried not to imagine how flushed her face must be. Embarrassment had flooded her senses to the point that she wasn't even aware of Megan's presence until the other woman stepped out into the aisle to great Adam.

"You must be the blue-eyed mechanic," Megan said as she extended her hand to him. He placed his shopping basket on the floor and shook her hand. "I'm Megan Walker, Katie's roommate."

"Adam Carey, Catherine's mechanic. It's nice to meet you, Megan." Adam looked up to see that Catherine was still shocked beyond words. She looked so adorable in her stunned state.

"Well, I have some shopping to do, so please excuse me," Megan said and disappeared down another aisle.

Catherine made a mental note to kill her when they got home. How could Megan leave her alone with this man, when she knew perfectly well that her best friend was completely incoherent around him? For several strained moments, she stared down at the floor, trying to concoct an explanation for her actions.

"Hi." Adam finally broke the silence.

Catherine nervously licked her parched lips and looked up at him. She could see he'd come straight from work. His shirt, which assumedly had once been white, was now grease-stained and blotchy. His blue jeans had seen better days but were relatively clean except for the almost black area around his thighs; obviously, his alternative to a grease rag.

"Hi," she answered simply.

Adam took in her humiliated composure and beet-red face, both of which made her look even more attractive.

"Christmas shopping?"

"Yes. I mean, no," Catherine stumbled as she looked at the clothing around her. "Megan and I were just looking." She could tell she was only digging herself deeper into a hole. She considered all-out retreat, but decided to change the subject instead. "How have you been?"

"Fine. How's your story coming?"

"To tell you the truth, I've come to a dead end. Aside from being extremely talented and intelligent, I don't think there's anything special about you." She gave him a smile to let him know that she was kidding.

"Is that so? I'm sorry to disappoint you, Katie."

Catherine felt a rush of air leave her lungs. Even the way he said her name left her feeling weak and defenseless.

"I've heard you can produce an amazing story from even the least interesting subjects," Adam said with a smile.

"Is that a challenge?"

"Only if you want it to be."

"I'd have to do another interview with unavoidable personal questions." Catherine gave him her best 'it's my way or the highway' look, but he wasn't about to be fooled.

"What makes you think I'll be any more revealing than before?" Adam asked as he crossed his strong arms. Toying with this beautiful woman's heart was wrong; he was the first to admit it. He had every intention of revealing his identity upon their next meeting, but until then he would make it his business to provide her with lasting memories.

"Believe me, Mr. Carey, I know there's a story bottled up inside, and I will do everything short of beating it out of you to get it."

Adam tipped his head to the side and studied her as if gauging her strength. With a grin he reached out and gently squeezed her arm.

"You may want to find an alternative to beating it out of me. I doubt there would be much contest."

Catherine opened her mouth to protest, but no words came forth. Adam's touch, as innocent as it had been, had paralyzed her. It was as if he knew it, too. His smile gave it away.

What Adam didn't give away was how amazed he was at her reaction to him. He knew that he was her exact opposite. His appearance was usually of no concern to him. His hands were seldom clean, due to the long hours of toil making a living. He had no idea why Catherine would be so attracted to a man like him, but for some reason she was. It was written all over her face.

"Well, if you still want me as your test subject, then I'll be waiting for your call to set up our next interview." Adam bent and picked up the basket. "I'll see you then, Katie."

"Goodbye," Catherine answered.

He turned to leave. The act was more of an escape than anything else. It was killing him to be near her and not act on his genuine emotions. He had taken only two steps when Catherine's voice stopped him.

"Adam,"

"Yes?" he asked as he turned back to her.

"It was nice seeing you again." Catherine's simple statement, or rather her tone, was filled with underlying questions.

"I know."

In two decisive words, his soothing tone covered all of her uncertainties. The only question left unanswered was why he didn't act on the affection that clearly showed in his eyes.

The awkward encounter left Catherine with a feeling of anticipation. Although she looked forward to their next meeting, she was also anxious about the outcome. Perhaps it was her levelheaded nature that caused her to second guess every situation and decision. As much as she wished to investigate Adam's motives, she still felt an obligation to Lyndon. Was it wrong to keep him on the line as a backup plan?

The entire scenario seemed unfair to her. Why, after being contently single for years, did she suddenly find herself caught in a maze created from two men's affections? It was complicated and exciting and scary.

"Is it safe to come back now?"

Catherine turned from her thoughts to find Megan comically hiding behind a rack of clothes.

"Yes. He's gone."

Megan came forth from her mock retreat shaking her head. "He looks rough, but he was all soft when he looked at you."

"What a coincidence. I seem to melt when I look at him." Catherine stared off in the direction of Adam's exit. "It was so kind of you to conveniently leave us alone in the most embarrassing moment of my life," she remarked sarcastically.

"I thought you would appreciate the privacy. Besides, I think you're more than capable of handling yourself. You are successfully keeping two men wrapped around your finger."

"I would prefer just one."

Megan smiled and suggested that they continue shopping. They walked the aisles side by side in silence, stopping only to point out a sale item or display.

"Which one?"

Catherine turned to her friend in confusion.

"Which one of what?"

"You said you'd prefer just one man wrapped around your finger. Which one would you prefer?"

"I don't know if I can answer that yet. Lyndon is open and promising, but Adam is shy and mysterious. It may be some time before I can or will have to choose."

"Tim is the easiest choice I ever made," Megan said with a sigh.

"You seem quite confident about it."

"I am right now."

Catherine nodded and began walking again. It was difficult to be happy for Megan when her relationship was based on emotion only. Without Christ as a foundation, any romance was sure to crumble.

Neither woman ended up spending much money on their designated shopping trip. Instead, they shared a great day of friendship and talking. To Catherine, that was far more rewarding than any bargain found in a store.

"I always thought it would be simple. I believed that the first initial eye contact would trigger something in my soul saying 'this is the one you were meant to be with'. But it's not at all like that. It's not like that with either of the two. One leaves me feeling confused and vulnerable, while the other offers me everything I need but don't want. Why does love require such effort? Isn't it that true, deep feeling that overcomes any attempt to hinder it? Is this obligation I feel to Lyndon a feeling to base a life on? How was it with you, Mom? What did you feel for Dad? Is it the same feeling you have now?"

"When I met your father he was an immature sixteen year old boy who thought he was a man. His constant nagging drove me crazy. Yet, there was always something deep in his eyes that made me wonder if there was more. I finally figured out that his teasing and jesting was his way of getting my attention. There was nothing he wouldn't say or do to get me to notice him. Somewhere along the line, it turned into affection. I found myself looking forward to every moment I could spend with him.

"One day I looked at him from across a crowded room and realized that there was no one else I'd rather share the rest of my life with but this man. He was still a boy in many ways, but it didn't matter to me. All that mattered was that we were in love. It wasn't the head-over-heels love I had expected. Your father was the only person I was completely comfortable with. He knew my every thought and spoke my words before I said them. His smile was enough to encourage me to take on the world. Now, I wake up to that same smile every morning.

"I can't tell you if your feelings are right or wrong, Katie. Only you know how you feel. I can tell you, though, to be in prayer about it. God's not going to lead you down the wrong path if you're in His will. Pray about your situation, and it will all work out. It may take time, and I know you feel frustrated right now to a point that you are desperate for answers. Don't be so desperate that you give up, or so desperate that you give in."

"And you say *I* have a way with words, Mom."

Lyndon twirled his ballpoint pen between his fingers and stared out the partition window at his favorite employee. Not only was Catherine his favorite, but she also gave him the most trouble. Not in what she did, but in what she didn't do. He knew better than to think that she would purposely lead him on. It was not the way she dressed that enticed him; she was always very modest in what she wore. Rather, it was who she *was* that captivated the young editor.

The distance between them was always a consistent arm's length. Sometimes Lyndon wondered if it was Catherine's unavailability that kept him interested. Of course, he would be overjoyed if she shared his feelings and they, as a couple, carried out their future accordingly. Yet, trying to capture her heart was like a thrill of suspense. With time, he was sure that she would see the potential he had to offer her. Until then, he would keep the same distance between them and obey all of the set boundaries. When Catherine was ready, he would only be an arm's length away.

Swipe by swipe, Catherine removed the powdery snow from her car's windshield. Winter had been releasing its fury for over a month now. Christmas had come and gone with unbelievable speed, and now the New Year was taking off full-throttle. Due to the cold weather and snow, her commute to work had become longer and starting her car was more of a leap of faith each day.

After verifying that enough snow was cleared off her windows for safe visibility, she made her way back into her house and allowed the car a few minutes to warm up. Megan was just making her way to the coffee pot and gave Catherine the best smile the morning could afford.

"Is that thermometer right?" Megan asked with a shudder.

"I don't know what the exact temperature is, but it's freezing out there."

Megan nodded in agreement, tapped on the thermometer, and then began filling the coffee filter with grounds.

"I'm going into Harrisville this afternoon," Megan said as she filled the pot with water. "Do you need anything?"

"Why are you going there?"

"I saw a job in the paper that looks interesting."

"A job? What's wrong with the one you have now?"

Megan didn't answer right away, and Catherine could see that something was wrong.

"It appears that my company prefers Christmas as the time to lay off their unwanted employees."

"Oh, Meg."

"It's okay," Megan insisted as she grabbed a mug from the cupboard. "They warned me this might happen. I just didn't expect it to be so soon. I've known all along that it would be temporary, but I didn't want to tell you."

"Why not?"

"Because you're so happy with your life right now. I don't want you feeling sorry for me. It was my irresponsibility that got me fired from the newspaper in the first place. I guess now I'm just dealing with the consequences."

Consequences?

Catherine had never heard that word from Megan before. In fact, this was the most sincere she had seen her in years. Perhaps she was softening. First Lyndon, now Megan; what was next?

"Just come back to the office, Meg. I'm sure that Lyndon still stands behind his offer."

"I don't know if I can work for him."

"He's changed, Meg. Everyone at the office would agree. If you think I'm partial, just ask any one of them."

Megan remained silent, and Catherine left her to think over her options. She was confident that she had said enough. The drive to work was practically relieving, due to the fact that Catherine had someone besides Adam or Lyndon to think about.

Megan found Adam under a lifted car, utilizing a wrench-like tool she'd never seen before. It took a while for him to notice that he had a visitor, so Megan took the opportunity to look him over. Her best friend had certainly not been exaggerating when she had said this man was attractive. From his shape, it was easy to see that he used his strength to make his living. Adam was by no means bulky, but he was sculpted. Megan found herself wishing Tim could look more like the mechanic in front of her.

As if he knew he was being daydreamed about, Adam looked out to find that he wasn't alone.

"Hello," he greeted Megan as he came out from under the car. "Megan, wasn't it?"

"Yes. Megan Walker."

Adam grabbed a grease rag and began wiping his hands. "Welcome to Carey's automotive. What brings you here?"

"I was in town, and I thought I'd stop by."

Adam smiled slightly and gave Megan a skeptical look. "Did Katie send you, by any chance?"

"No. In fact, I'd prefer if she didn't know I was here."

"Why so secretive?"

"This may sound strange, but I wanted to observe you."

"Yes, that does sound strange." Adam agreed.

"I'm a journalist, Mr. Carey. Observing is what I do best. I have an ability to notice things that others may not."

"Like what?"

"Well, for one, you don't use a rag to clean your hands; you use it for a distraction." She pointed to the filthy rage in his hands. "Some people twirl their pens, and some fiddle with their tie-tack. You obviously use the front of your jeans to wipe the grease and grime off your hands. That rag is only a diversion to prevent meaningful conversation."

Adam nodded slowly and tossed the rag onto the workbench. "I'm impressed. Do you read palms, too?" he kidded her.

Megan smiled briefly but returned to the previous subject.

"Katie is my best friend. I don't want her to get hurt."

"What do you mean by that?"

She didn't answer. Adam waited for several seconds but to no avail.

"It was nice to see you again, Mr. Carey."

Megan turned and was out the door before Adam could speak. *I don't want to see her hurt, either,* he thought as he watched Megan's car pull away. *That's why I'm standing here instead of running to Katie.*

"I'm glad you called, Carey," John said as he took a seat in Adam's office. He was Adam's closest friend and mentor. "It's been too long since we've had a conversation to ourselves."

Adam smiled in agreement and set a cup of coffee in front of his guest, the man he respected like a father. Although Adam's own father and mother lived only thirty miles away, they did not share his faith. That barrier always made it difficult for Adam to speak on a personal level with his father. At this time, he needed advice from another Christian man. John had to pass by the shop on his way home, so Adam had felt no guilt in asking him to stop by.

"How is Ashley?" Adam inquired after John's wife of five years.

"She's fine, but I don't think you called me here to talk about her."

Adam nodded and took a sip of his coffee.

"You know me well, John."

"Yes, I do. I know how you keep things to yourself. Whatever it is you want to talk about has probably been weighing on your mind for some time."

Once again, Adam nodded.

"Is there such a thing as holy covetousness? I mean, I've heard of holy anger, but what about coveting?"

"I don't know. I guess it depends on the circumstance."

"If you want something so pure and beautiful that you can't have, but still want, is that a sin?"

"It would help me if I knew what you were talking about."

"I met the most amazing woman."

John immediately got a concerned look on his face.

"If she's married, then you're…"

"She's not married," Adam clarified. "I could sit here until midnight telling you what I adore about her, but it wouldn't do any good. All that matters is that I can't make her mine."

"Why not?"

"Her name is Catherine Scott--she's Jesse Scott's older sister."

John raised his brows in surprise. He hadn't expected this. Adam *did* have an unusual case on his hands.

"Does she know?"

"No. To her, I'm just the mechanic who fixed her car. It would be so much easier if she was off limits, but she looks at me the same way I look at her. I think she cares, but I can't make a move to take things any further. I have to sit on these emotions. It's killing me."

Adam raked his hands through his hair and sighed. John watched him for several moments, trying to completely comprehend the intensity of his friend's feelings. Adam Carey was not the type to get flustered. He rarely ever showed any feeling at all. It wasn't that he was stubborn or proud; he was just private.

"So many times I wish I could go back to that day, John. I wish I had done more."

"You know it wasn't your fault."

"That doesn't make the pain go away. It just sits there idle until I look into Katie's eyes. Right now, she looks at me in a way that no other woman has ever looked at me before, but if I tell her that I'm responsible for Jesse's death, she'll never look at me the same again. I can't stand that thought. What am I supposed to do?"

"You could never tell her and live a lie, or you could tell her right away and set things straight."

"I was afraid you'd say that."

John smiled at his friend and begged God to give him guidance. A choice had to be made, and it was going to be a hard one.

Chapter Eight

Megan walked up the familiar flight of stairs to the second story, but nothing was familiar about the unsettling feelings inside of her. In her opinion, she had never lowered herself to this level before. Her life, in its entirety, had always revolved around her. Every subject or situation was determined by *her* wants, making it extraordinary that she was even here.

The walk across the office went much too fast. In seconds, she could see the dreaded Mr. Reinhardt through his window shades. He was seated in his chair, facing the street-side window with the rough-draft paper sprawled in front of him. When Megan reached his office, without taking a chance to back out of her decision, she gently knocked on the doorjamb. Lyndon, looking as aristocratically handsome as she remembered, turned and gave her a surprised smile.

"Megan. I was hoping you'd stop by."

Megan winced at the sour feelings his voice aroused.

"I'd like my job back, Lyndon," she told him frankly. "I'm not the begging type, so I'm only going to ask once."

Lyndon slowly folded the newspaper and neatly placed it on his desk.

"I run a disciplined department full of deadlines and headlines, Megan. When people belong here, they stay here. There is seldom a dull moment or time enough to ponder over personal problems. Being late cannot be tolerated." He stopped and studied her face to determine if she understood him. With a defeated nod of her head, she turned toward the door.

"Miss Walker, you forgot your assignment."

Megan turned slowly to find him extending a piece of paper to her.

"It's due by three."

With complete understanding, she took the indicated paper and left the room without uttering a word. Lyndon took a moment to think about the second chance he had just given his unruly employee. For once, he had been firm but forgiving. It truly gave him a sense of accomplishment that he owed solely to Catherine. He made a mental note to tell her.

What bothers me the most is that four months ago I didn't have anyone. Previously, the only voice I had inside my head was my own. Now, I have the smooth voice of Adam Carey. And when Adam isn't speaking to me, Lyndon is. If security was my main goal, I would look no further than him. He has all that there is to offer.

Although I do want security and the feeling of being safe and taken care of, what I want even more is the non-materialistic security that comes from being loved.

So, now I find myself back at the beginning again. I'm trapped between two extraordinary men. One offers me everything I need, and the other unknowingly offers me everything I want and desire.

"Catherine, wake up."

Megan gently tapped her friend's shoulder and looked down at her in concern. She'd never seen Catherine this way. It wasn't unusual for Megan to occasionally fall asleep during the earlier hours at the office, but not Catherine. She was always alert and on her toes.

"I wasn't sleeping," Catherine tried to reason as she raised her head from where it had been resting in her hands.

"Yeah, right. What exactly do you call what you were just doing?"

Catherine just shrugged her shoulders in defeat. "What are you doing here?"

"As of two hours ago, I'm the newspaper's newest employee," Megan said with pride.

"I must say that I'm proud of you, Meg. That must have taken some guts."

"It took some persuasion, but I told myself that it was something I had to do. I walked into that office and was shocked. Catherine, you've done a miracle with that man."

"What do you mean by that?"

"He's not the same as he was two months ago. When he came here he was the most inconsiderate, arrogant man I'd ever seen, but not anymore. He still puts on the tough act, but underneath it all you can see that he's broken in. I think he owes it all to you."

"Don't start liking him now, Megan. I may have to get jealous," Catherine kidded her.

"Don't worry. A church boy like that is not my type."

Catherine smiled but thought silently, *I pray that it is someday, Meg.*

Josh, this is Catherine. She'll be shadowing me today…

Josh, this is Catherine Scott. She's doing some research with me…

Josh, this is my friend, Katie. I want to marry her but can't bring myself to tell her the truth…

As Adam mulled each introduction over in his head, he began to wonder what he had gotten himself into inviting Catherine to spend a day with him at the shop. In ten minutes, Josh Mitchell was bringing his wife's car in for repair, and Katie was due at the shop any second. Adam thought back over their conversation from the day before.

"I figure now that the holidays are over it would be a good time to continue our interview."

"Instead of an interview, could I just come and watch you with your daily routine?"

"Sure. I can't promise that it will be exciting, but you are more than welcome to stop by."

"I'll be there at eight then."

Having someone looking over his shoulder as he worked wasn't Adam's first preference, but if someone had to do it, Catherine was certainly a pleasant candidate. No doubt she would be dressed in her office attire, with her blonde hair wound tightly in a bun and her notebook crooked beneath her arm. Chances are, she'd look wonderful, and Adam would be distracted all day.

The words John had told him were fresh in his mind, and he seriously considered confronting the truth, as ugly as it was, today with Katie. If she hated him for it, he wouldn't blame her. But, if by some miracle, she chose to forgive him, he would welcome the clean slate with open arms.

The office door opened and the subject of his thoughts entered the room, accompanied by a surge of cold January air. Catherine wasted no time in closing the door and turned back to find Adam smiling at her.

"Hi."

"Hi."

Both individuals stared at each other as if contemplating their next move. It was awkward in a sense, but also completely comfortable.

Catherine had awakened early and had spent the last two hours guessing the day's events. She had every question, every expression, and every response planned perfectly in her mind, but she knew every pre-formed thought would flee the moment she stepped into this office. As it turned out, she hit the nail straight on the head. All she could see was the smile on Adam's face, and all she could wonder was why she was feeing this way.

Adam was wondering why he *had* to feel the way he did. If it were anyone else, he would go about the day in normal fashion. But this wasn't just anyone, this was Katie. Katie would be looking over his shoulder for the next eight hours, and it was going to drive him crazy. Not only was she a beautiful distraction, but she was also a trigger for memories and questions that he did not want surfaced. It was too late to turn back now. She was standing in his office and he had willingly invited her there. Business had to continue as usual.

"Would you like me to take your coat, Katie?" Adam suggested.

"Yes, thank you." Catherine watched as he draped her jacket over one of the office chairs.

"Josh Mitchell is my first customer," Adam began. "His wife hit a deer a week ago, and he's bringing her car in for body work. He should be here in a second."

"You must have a lot of repairs like that around here."

"Yes, that's true. In upstate New York, you don't hit deer; they hit you."

Catherine laughed at the truth in his humor.

"How did you manage to get the entire day off just to come and watch me work?"

"You may have forgotten, but this is a genuine assignment. I intend to work on this as I would any other article."

"I hope you find enough to write about. You may have to resort to making up fictitious facts just to fill in the empty gaps."

"That won't be necessary. This shop alone is potential enough for a great story, not to mention the man behind it."

Adam shook his head but smiled shyly. She was at it again, making him feel remarkably full of purpose. There was nothing romantic about the way she encouraged him, yet that only added to the already abundant list of her attractive and praise-worthy characteristics.

How do you expect me to tell you the truth when you act so wonderfully?

"It sounds like your first customer is here."

Adam looked out the window at Josh getting out of the family car. He hadn't even heard a car pull up.

Get a grip, Carey. She's just a woman. And besides, you can't have her anyway. That little reminder was just what Adam needed to get his feet back on the ground. His heart was supposed to be filled with Christ's love, not the obsession with another human being.

"Excuse me," he said as he scooted by Catherine and opened the door. "Go ahead and pull the car in, Josh."

"Sure thing, Carey," Catherine heard the other man answer.

Adam closed the door and stepped into the shop bay. As he held the button to open the overhead door, he looked over at Catherine.

"Time to get to work, Katie. Grab your notebook. You're about to experience just how uneventful my job really is."

Catherine knew it wasn't true but nodded and followed Adam's directions. Seconds later, a mangled sedan was parked in the bay, and she was about to be introduced to the owner. The very moment Adam had practiced in his mind was upon him, but he couldn't remember which introduction he had decided on. Mr. Mitchell got out of the car, took one look at Catherine, then turned to Adam with a mischievous smile.

"You didn't tell me you had a girlfriend."

Adam opened his mouth to protest, but Josh was already speaking to Catherine.

"I've known Carey from the day he started working with his uncle Joe, but he fails to tell me that he's got a woman in his life. I can't say that I blame him, though." He gave her a wink and quickly ran his eyes over her frame.

Adam saw the act and felt a need to step in and protect her.

"Don't worry, Katie," he said as he gave Josh a stern look. "He's harmless *and* married."

"Oh, that's right," Josh said and turned his attention to the car. "What do you think of that, Carey? Darned deer ran right into my wife. She didn't see it coming until it came through the side window."

"It certainly did some damage," Adam noted as he looked over the car.

"That's for sure. If it were anyone else, I wouldn't expect this thing back for a few weeks, but I know you'll have it done in a snap." Josh complemented Adam and then turned to Catherine. "This here's the best mechanic you'll find for a hundred miles, but I'm sure you already know that," he added with a sly grin. The sound of a horn drew his attention. "That's my ride. I'll see you two later."

When he had closed the door behind him, Adam shook his head and chuckled.

"Is he always so unambiguous?" Catherine was still surprised by the man's quirky behavior.

"I don't really know what that word means, but yes. Josh is one of my most loyal customers, but I must say that sometimes he takes it a little too far."

"I don't think *you* took it far enough."

"I'm sorry, I don't follow."

"You weren't in any hurry to clarify that I'm not your girlfriend."

The words hadn't come out the way she'd wanted, but there was no taking them back now. All she had wanted to do was acknowledge the fact that Adam had shown no sign of setting Josh straight. Instead, he seemed to bask in the role playing.

"I completely agree with you, Katie, but to deny it only would have added fuel to his fire."

"I guess I'll take your word for it. After all, you do know him better than I."

"All right. How about we get to work then?"

For the next three hours Catherine sat to the side as she watched Adam display his master craftsmanship. Each tool was selected carefully and then used with precision. He would stop occasionally, but only to briefly explain what he was doing and take a sip of his coffee. When lunchtime rolled around, he offered to take her to the sandwich shop down the street. Once they had taken their seats, Catherine asked him one of the questions on her list.

"Do you ever get tired of your job?"

"I don't think I know of anyone who doesn't occasionally get sick of their job. Sometimes it happens to me, but when I'm not working, I find myself looking for something to fix. I like fixing things and watching them work."

"You're a peacemaker, then."

"I'm not sure I'd put it that way. I just like using tools and enjoying the outcome."

"To me that says, for example, that if you had been in an argument, you would be the first to reconcile, even if it wasn't your fault, just to clear the air. Seems to me that you don't like things being chaotic or messy. You like things neat and tidy, whether it is your workbench or your personal life. Am I wrong?"

"On the contrary, you're quite right. I don't like confrontation."

"That's why you work alone. With only you, there's no one to disagree with. Sure, you have customers in and out daily, but they're not an active part of your life."

"Are you saying I'm antisocial?"

"No. I'm just trying to get an idea of what kind of personality you really do have. From what I can tell so far, you're respected amongst everyone you know, and no one speaks badly of you. In fact, you are recommended because of your honesty. That's something to be proud of, Adam. Don't be ashamed that you like to work alone. I wish I had that opportunity for myself."

"Why don't you take it?"

"Take what?"

"The opportunity. You're a good writer. If you want to work alone, then do it. There are plenty of opportunities out there for someone with your talent. From what I've heard, you write one mean story. You could use that in other places. You could edit or just write freelance. If you want to, then just step out on your own. The chances are there, Katie. You just have to go for them."

"That may be something I'd like to pursue someday, but for now I'm secure in my job. I love it. I really do. I love it because of times like right now, when I can dig deep into someone's life until I have enough intriguing information to create an amazing puzzle. Everyone likes a good puzzle, don't you think?"

"What if the puzzle doesn't turn out the way they had hoped?"

Catherine was confused by his question, but thought it over for a second and then gave an answer.

"No doubt they still enjoyed and learned from putting the puzzle together."

Unknowingly, she had struck a chord in Adam's heart. He stared blankly down at his plate, trying to swallow the hurt that was welling up inside. He knew that Catherine had feelings for him. He knew it without a doubt. He could practically feel it from across the table. But, he was going to break her heart. This entire relationship, from its beginning, had been a ticking bomb--and he held the detonator in his hand.

"My life is a complicated puzzle, Katie, and I'm afraid you won't like the outcome when all the pieces are put together. For that reason, I think this should be our last interview. You are running out of legitimate questions to ask me. I think you've always had enough information to write your story. Let's stop pretending that our encounters are strictly business."

Catherine was speechless after hearing Adam's attempted explanation. She was disappointment beyond words that he had no interest in taking things further. Without a word, she retrieved some bills and laid them on the table to cover her half of lunch. After gathering her purse, she stood and looked down at the man who had just stomped on her heart.

"If I have all that I need to write this story, then there is no need for me to spend the afternoon asking you questions that you have no answers for. Thank you for your time, Adam. I enjoyed it, even if you didn't."

Catherine walked from the restaurant, praying that he would not follow her. Her heart was so fragile that the sight of him would be enough to send her over the edge. She reached her car, thankful that she had offered to drive and not caring that Adam would have to walk back to his shop. She fumbled with her keys in the biting cold and finally was able to unlock and open her door, only to see a hand come from behind and push it shut. She turned and found herself pinned between her car and Adam's white tee shirt.

"You're wrong, Catherine. I did enjoy it. Every second from that first day at the shop right up until now, I've loved every moment. But while loving every minute, I was also hating not telling you how I feel."

"I'm so confused, Adam," she confessed, feeling her throat close with emotion. *Why didn't you--why don't you tell me? Can't you see that I'm crazy for you?*

"It's better this way, I promise."

"You don't have any feelings for me?"

Adam looked down at this amazing woman who looked too fragile to touch but begged to be held. The bitter air induced her shivering, and her bottom lip quivered ever so slightly.

"Katie, I can't explain."

"Then don't. Don't say a thing."

Catherine challenged him with her stare. Her face was full of hurt, but as usual her eyes told the real story. They told him that she was putting it all on the line. She refused to be the one who would walk away with regrets. Adam's hands on the car behind her created the perfect barrier of security, and she wasn't going to break it until he did some explaining.

"I don't want to break your heart," he said in a hushed voice.

"You already have," Catherine whispered back through the cold air. "You've broken my heart and left me more confused than I can say."

"Katie," Adam began and then realized that there was only one way to end this the right way. "Goodbye, Katie," he whispered and then bent his head low. He hesitated only a second when he heard a helpless breath leave her lips and then gave her the most innocent, gentle kiss she had ever received. When he pulled back, he looked at the single tear that was making its way down her cheek. "I'm so sorry."

Catherine somehow knew he was not speaking of the kiss as she watched him make his way back into the restaurant without another word. Suddenly, she realized she was freezing. She climbed into her car and turned over the engine. Somehow she managed to make it all the way back to her house before reality set in. She fought back the tears as she made her way up the sidewalk. Once inside the door, she leaned her back against it and a sob escaped her lips. The harder she tried to stifle the tears, the more violent her crying became. When her legs could hold her no longer, she slid down the door and landed in a heap on the floor. She brought her knees to her chest and hugged them with the last of her strength. Not since Jesse's death had she cried this hard.

"I don't understand, Lord," she whispered in between sobs. "It hurts so badly. Why would you let me be lured into these feelings only to have them end like this?" She continued to cry until all her strength was gone, and she fell asleep to dream about the feel of Adam's lips on her own.

Adam was just about to give up when he saw Lyndon walking from desk to desk handing a piece of paper to each of his employees. As Adam walked over, Lyndon just finished with one of the journalist and looked up at him in surprise.

"Carey,"

"Hi, Lyndon. Is Katie here?"

"To my knowledge, she was spending the day with you."

"That was the plan, but she left early. Do you know where she is? I need to talk to her."

It wasn't until that moment that Lyndon realized how out of sorts Adam was.

"What happened, Carey?"

"It's a long story. Right now, I have to find her. Can you tell me where she lives?"

"That's not such a good idea," Lyndon said rather firmly.

"Why not?"

"I don't want her getting hurt by you anymore than she already has."

Adam took in the protective glare that Lyndon was giving him. Catherine had told him that she and Lyndon weren't dating, but she had never mentioned what kind of feelings Lyndon had for her.

"You love her, don't you?" Adam voiced aloud.

"And you don't?" Lyndon threw back cynically.

Both men stared at each other but remained silent. Adam hated being in the heat of a discussion such as this, so of course, he was the first to give in and speak.

"I just need to talk to her and explain."

"Explain what? Explain why you keep giving her the false hope of a relationship and then stealing it away from her over and over again? I'd like to hear that explanation myself."

"I don't want to fight about this."

"I'm not fighting," he clarified and then continued. "Do you have any idea what you've put her through? Every time you crushed her, she would end up in my office trying to understand you. Tell me, Carey, what is it that makes you push her away, when all she wants is to be with you?"

Adam had no idea how to explain why he purposely had kept from having a relationship with Katie.

"Or maybe you just don't want a future with her at all," Lyndon suggested.

"This isn't about our future. It's about our past." Adam paused only a moment before turning and making his way out of the office. Lyndon told himself that it was none of his business, but something inside told him that Catherine had been right: Adam Carey did have a secret. What she hadn't known was that it involved her.

When the office finally emptied and Lyndon was alone, he sat behind his computer and went to work. It had been a while since he had played the part of a journalist, but he still remembered all the tricks of the trade. He began with the basics. Catherine was first. He examined everything he could dig up, yet nothing stood out from the pages. Such was not the case with Adam Carey. After typing his name, Lyndon was referred to the Malone local newspaper archives. This seemed odd to him. He knew that Catherine had grown up in Malone, but if Adam had as well, then she would have known him somehow.

The article bearing Adam's name had nothing to do with the town of Malone but rather with one of its factories. The story told of Adam's involvement in a fatal accident at the local machine shop. It certainly was a devastating story, but the real shock came about halfway through the page. The paper only listed one fatality: Jesse Scott. That name jumped off the page with astounding clarity.

Lyndon stared at the page, trying to decipher the article. Did this mean that Adam had been responsible for Jesse's death? It must have been deemed an accident or else he would have been charged with manslaughter. It didn't explain why he wouldn't tell Catherine who he was.

Maybe there was more to the story. The weekend was just around the corner, and Lyndon was going to Malone for some research. Until then, he wasn't going to speak a word of this to Catherine. The truth would reveal itself when the time was right.

Chapter Nine

Surprisingly, Catherine got a good night's sleep and was looking quite refreshed when she arrived at work on Friday morning. Nothing about the way she acted was abnormal; however, Lyndon's constant eye upon her was making her feel uneasy.

During the morning meeting, she purposely avoided eye-contact with her boss, but Megan kept her sight trained on the man at the head of the table. He didn't take his eyes off Catherine for more than ten seconds. His behavior was peculiar, to put it mildly.

Resorting to her morning meeting habits from the days when Mr. Cady was boss, Megan scribbled a note and passed it to Catherine during a moment when Mr. Reinhardt wasn't looking.

What's with Lyndon staring at you?

Catherine quickly read the note and then turned to Megan and shrugged. She had no idea what was fueling his strange behavior, but she would be sure to ask him when the meeting was over.

As it turned out, Lyndon disappeared for the rest of the day. Whether he was working with one of the other employees or just plain hiding, Catherine didn't know. It wasn't until the end of the business day that she finally found him alone in his office. She knocked gently on the doorjamb and waited for him to look up at her.

"I thought everyone had gone home," he said. "Who else is here?"

"It's just me," she answered as she walked into the office and fell into the chair across from him. "And you."

Lyndon nodded and pretended to straighten the papers on his desk. He didn't like keeping things from Catherine, so it was difficult to act like there wasn't anything on his mind. Another pressure was that she had pointed out, innocently enough, that they were alone. Something in that declaration made him feel uneasy. It wasn't that he was uncomfortable around her. What worried him was that he was too comfortable with her.

"Busy day?" she asked.

"Typical Friday."

"What are your plans for the weekend?"

You just had to ask, he thought. "I'm going up north for an interview."

Catherine made no attempt to hide her surprise.

"You're doing a story?"

"No. This is more like 'personal research.' I'll be back in time for church on Sunday." Lyndon couldn't stand that he had to tiptoe around the truth, but it did give him a glimpse of how Carey must feel. "What about you? Any big plans?"

"Just relaxing. I need some peace and quiet."

"Sounds like a great plan to me."

For a few moments, there was silence. Catherine watched as Lyndon's eyes roamed about the room as if he hoped to find a change of subject hanging on the wall. She wished he would offer some type of explanation for his rather protective behavior, but instead he posed an unusual question.

"You know how I feel, right, Cat?"

"About what?"

"About you."

"I guess."

"That's not good enough. I want you to be sure."

"Why is this suddenly so important, and how is it relevant?"

"It's very relevant. I don't care if I look like a fool or if you think I'm crazy, or both. I don't want you to leave without knowing how I feel."

"How do you feel, Lyndon?"

Catherine watched him tense at her question, but she didn't back down. He had brought up the subject, after all.

"Confessing isn't going to change anything," he rationalized. "It will only make you feel guilty and pity my helpless state."

"Are you really so proud that you can't tell me?"

Lyndon stood and went to the door where his jacket was hanging on the coat rack and began to put it on.

"If you already know, then that's good enough for now."

Catherine did feel guilty that she owned this man's affections, but she wasn't about to give in or forget the bittersweet feelings she had for Adam. As Lyndon walked his favorite journalist to her car, he didn't force any conversation. Instead, he simply wished her a good weekend and went on his way, praying that he was wrong about her connection with Adam Carey.

"Officer Daniels will see you now, Mr. Reinhardt."

Lyndon stood and followed the receptionist across the waiting room and down a narrow hallway to a small office.

"Thank you for seeing me on such short notice, Officer," Lyndon greeted the other man with a firm handshake.

"Not a problem. I'll be happy to answer any questions you may have."

"Well, as you know, I'm doing some research on the fatality at the machine shop four years ago. Would it be possible for me to see the accident report?"

"Sure. I can't let you take it with you or copy it, but you're welcome to read it over." Officer Daniels walked from the room and returned shortly with a folder that he handed to Lyndon. At first glance, the contents seemed like a huge collaboration of gibberish with no sense of order, but after studying it for several seconds Lyndon began to comprehend some of it.

"You were the officer in charge of the investigation?"

"Yes, although there wasn't much to investigate. I did the usual: take some pictures, interview the witnesses, and thoroughly document the scene."

Lyndon continued to skim through the pages before coming to a halt. Carey's name appeared at the top of one page and was followed by a paragraph of what happened that day in his own words.

"This Adam Carey...do you remember him?"

"I sure do. He was so shaken that it took me half an hour to get his statement. He had tried to save that Scott boy but couldn't. I think he blamed himself for it, although it wasn't anyone's fault."

Lyndon read over Adam's statement and the statement given by the other man at the scene. The stories coincided up to the point where the forklift driver had gone for help, leaving Adam with Jesse. Only one observation troubled Lyndon: Jesse was able to breathe and speak when the driver went for help but was dead when he returned. Without a doubt, something had to have taken place in those minutes. The statements were unrevealing, leaving only one place to find the answer he was looking for.

"Thank you for your time, Officer," Lyndon said as he stood and handed the folder back to the uniformed man across the desk. "I appreciate you taking time to see me and answer my questions."

"I'm glad I could help. Have a safe trip back to Star Lake."

Lyndon shook his hand and turned to leave. He had another stop to make. This time he wasn't going as a journalist. He was going as Lyndon Reinhardt, the man in love with Catherine Scott.

It was nearly dark by the time Lyndon made it into Harrisville. Having only an address made it difficult to find his destination. The town was surprisingly quiet for a Saturday evening, allowing him to travel slowly along the roads without backing up traffic. At last, he found the street he had been looking for, and shortly thereafter, he was knocking on the door of Adam Carey's house.

Looking relaxed in a pair of gym shorts and sweatshirt, Adam answered the door, surprised to find Lyndon standing on the step.

"Lyndon, come in out of the cold," he offered and watched the other man closely as he entered the warm house. "What are you doing here? Is something wrong?"

"I need to know," Lyndon paused only to cup his hands over his mouth and blow warm air across them, "why you haven't told Catherine who you are."

"You know?"

"Yes, but she doesn't. I want to know why not."

Adam took a seat on the living room's only sofa and looked up at his unexpected guest. "I've taken so much from her already. I can't possibly hurt her more. She deserves better than me."

"No. What she deserves is to hear the truth from the only one who seems to know it. I can't believe you think she's better off not knowing."

"She *is* better off. I ended our correspondence for that very reason."

"You actually think it's that easy? She's not going to wake up tomorrow and just forget she ever met you. It doesn't happen that way, not when you've got a hold on her like you do."

Adam stood and walked across the small room until he was face-to-face with Lyndon.

"I need to ask you a question. Do you think that my telling her will drive her right back into your arms?" Adam's voice was soft and not at all accusing.

"That's not why I'm here. I want you to tell her because I love her. I loved her before you came into her life, and I'll love her still when this is over."

"How do you expect this to end, Lyndon? It's obvious to me. I don't deserve Katie just as much as I can't provide what she needs. I give up! She belongs with you."

"But she's in love with you!"

Adam was caught completely off guard by this statement, but he did his best not to show it.

"That's reason enough for me to keep my distance. No doubt she'd hate me if she knew the truth."

Lyndon drew a long breath, trying to keep the disappointment from his face. "I'm sorry you feel that way, Carey. I came here to give you the opportunity to be the one to tell her, but since you refuse to, I'll do it."

Adam didn't protest as Lyndon let himself out. He just stared at the door in disbelief. Catherine Scott loved him! He was determined to bask in that fact for the next few minutes. When the revelation was complete, he would no longer hold the key to her heart.

Ashley Warner opened the front door to find her husband's friend waiting patiently on the front step.

"Hi, Ashley. Is John here?" Adam asked and accepted her invitation inside.

"He is. I'll get him." Ashley made her way to the den where her husband was working at putting together his new entertainment center. "Honey, Carey's here to see you. He looks kind of, um, preoccupied."

"I'll be right there." John placed his screwdriver on the coffee table, walked past his wife, and made his way to the living room. Ashley wisely stayed behind, knowing that the men would need privacy.

"What's going on, Carey?"

"I'm sorry to stop in uninvited, but I need some advice."

"Sure. Sit down."

"It's about Catherine. Her boss found out about my involvement in Jesse's death, and he's going to tell her. I agree with him that she should hear it from me, but I also told her goodbye. I don't intend to bother her again."

"So, you would like to know if I think you should tell her yourself?"

"Yes."

"Well, I think you've already found your answer."

"Lyndon, I've decided that I won't be finishing my article on Adam."

The rehearsed lines that Lyndon had chosen to use to tell Catherine about Adam vanished. He had planned to sit beside her and gently tell her the story. He never dreamed that she would be the one to bring up the subject.

"I think you should finish it, Cat."

"I can't. This isn't just any story."

"I know. That's why you should see it through." Lyndon hadn't planned on having this conversation in church, but felt that now was as good a time as any to tell her. People were chatting all around them while others were making their way to their cars. Praying that they wouldn't be interrupted, Lyndon began his explanation.

"You saw more in Carey than meets the eye, and you insisted he was story material. As it turns out, you were right. The problem is that the story involves you."

"What are you talking about?"

"The day Jesse died, Adam was there."

"What?"

"He was picking up a delivery, and Jesse was helping when the chain snapped. It hit Adam in the face, and the box landed on your brother."

"Are you saying that Adam's responsible?"

"I'm just telling you what I know."

"What if I don't believe you?"

"One of the benefits of being an editor is that it doesn't take much prodding to have an accident report handed over to you."

The seriousness in his tone caused a familiar numbness to steal over Catherine's body. It was the same feeling she had received the moment she had learned of Jesse's death. Now it was like she was reliving that moment, with all of its pain.

Lyndon watched as she stifled her emotions. He hated seeing her in pain like this. Why hadn't Carey ever told her? So much hurt could have been saved if he had told the truth from the beginning. It was too late to reconcile now. The damage had been done. Carey had successfully shattered Catherine's heart, and now Lyndon set about picking up the pieces.

"I'm sorry it had to turn out this way, Cat."

"I must look like such a fool." She tried to smile even as tears stung her eyes. "You must think I'm a hopeless case."

"That's not true."

"I'm going home."

Her abruptness took Lyndon by surprise, but he understood if she wasn't up to talking. Catherine stood and began walking toward the door.

"If you need anything," Lyndon offered, "let me know. I want to help."

"Thanks," she replied automatically and then left the building.

As much as he wanted to go after her, Lyndon remained standing in the aisle. His aggressive care wouldn't do anything but drive her away. The best thing he could do right now was just be a friend.

An unfamiliar truck pulling into the drive caused Megan to wonder if Catherine was expecting someone. She turned from the window and hollered down the hallway.

"Cat?"

Silence was her only answer. The soft hum of water running in the shower told her that Catherine wouldn't be accepting any visitors. Besides, it was seven-thirty in the morning; who would be coming to see either of them?

"Adam Carey," Megan said as she opened the front door

"Hello, Megan," the rough, but good-looking mechanic greeted her through the cold. "Is Katie here?"

"It's probably best if you not speak to her."

"That's why I *need* to speak to her. I need to explain."

"That's all right. Lyndon already did the explaining for you."

"That may be, but he wasn't there that day. He doesn't know the whole story."

"The whole story, Adam," Megan began as she stepped outside and closed the door behind her to keep the voices from traveling, "goes like this: you let her believe that you were *Mr. Right,* and she fell head-over-heels. In the back of her mind, though, she always wondered why you wouldn't make the first move. It troubled her that you remained somehow unattainable. So, naturally, she began to think it was something she had, or hadn't, done. While she was trying to decipher you, she had the constant pressure of Lyndon's affections. I've never liked the man personally, but I'll give him credit for one thing: at least he let his feelings be known."

"I'm not a coward, Megan. I just wanted to protect her. The sooner she distanced herself from me, the better. How could she ever love the man who killed her only brother? It's not possible."

"Then why are you here?"

"I'm here because I found in Catherine what I'd been missing all my life. Although she'll never feel the same for me, I at least owe her an explanation for what happened both four years ago and in the last few months."

"I admire that, but I don't think she's ready to hear any of it. I still think it's best if you leave."

Adam hesitated, but had to agree that Catherine needed her space. He told Megan goodbye and made his way to his truck. Megan went back inside, closed the door behind her and heard the sound of the shower. It had been difficult to tell Adam no, but she was confident that in the long run it would be for the best.

The change in Catherine was as unavoidable as it was depressing. Inwardly, Lyndon had hoped that she would snap out of her fantasy and see that he was very real and very capable of supplying for her every need. By no means was she cold or curt to him, but neither was she drawn to him in her self-enveloping state. The stories she produced were just as interesting as they'd always been, but the dreamy look in her eyes was gone, taking with it some of her vigor.

Time after time, she told herself to get on with her life. The convinced attitude never lasted long enough, though. Her days were spent working harder than ever, trying to lead her co-workers, as well as her boss, to believe that she was all right. At night, she would lay awake suppressing the tears that wanted so badly to come until the efforts exhausted her, and she fell asleep. It occurred to her that she might need some time off, but that would just show everyone how incapable she was.

Work became her escape. She became so diligent that it was frightening, even to her. Lyndon waited patiently for the right time to confront her, but most days she was so distant that he thought it impossible to carry on a conversation. His chance finally arrived one evening when all the employees were gone. He stepped from his office and secured the door behind him. Catherine was still present though, seated at her desk, fingers flying over the keyboard.

Seeing that she was distracted and wanting to get her attention, he reached over her and turned the computer monitor off. Catherine swiveled in her chair and tried to look angry.

"I was working, Lyndon!"

"You're not fooling me."

"What?"

"You may have everyone else, including you, convinced, but you're not fooling me."

"It's very chivalrous of you, but I don't need a hero."

"I know. What you need is a man who loves you and wants nothing more than to take care of you."

"I thought I had that in Adam, but all I had was a lie." Catherine looked past her boss, fighting back the memories. "I can't believe I was so blind. Everything pointed me to the truth, but I was too captivated to see it. He just kept leading me deeper and deeper into the dark, and I never stopped to ask why he acted so strange or why he kept his distance. On top of that, there's the way I treated you through the whole ordeal."

"You've never done anything to me worth fretting over," Lyndon interrupted her.

"It's what I *haven't* done that makes me feel awful. How could you possibly care for someone who is so immature with her feelings?"

Lyndon didn't answer right away. Instead, he looked at Catherine until she met his gaze.

"How I feel," he began slowly, "has nothing to do with what you have or haven't done, Cat. As for immaturity, I recall you accusing me of being childish on many occasions. The rest of the office would agree with you."

For the first time since the conversation began, Catherine smiled. It was subtle, but Lyndon caught it.

"Let's go, Miss Scott. I'll walk you to your car."

Catherine didn't argue; she was too emotionally drained to. She was halfway home before she realized how nice it had been to talk to Lyndon.

"Do you think we could have Carey over for dinner?"

Those had been John Warner's words to his wife one week ago, and now Ashley was putting the finishing touches on the meal she had prepared for their guest.

John had noticed the unusual countenance of his friend on Sunday morning. By the evening service, he had arranged to have him over for dinner the following week. Adam had been glad to accept the offer. The past week had been a long one--not due to an overbooked schedule, but because concentration was nearly impossible. Katie was on his mind constantly, and when he wasn't thinking about her smile or the smell of her perfume, he was begging the Lord to take away the heart-wrenching feelings that he still had for her.

John and Ashley weren't expecting him until six, but Adam figured they wouldn't mind if he showed up a little early. He assumed correctly and was welcomed warmly into their house at five-thirty.

"Carey! Come in! Let me take your coat."

Adam thanked John and removed his shoes, while the other man found a place on the rack for his coat.

"Is work keeping you busy enough?"

"It's about normal for this time of year," Adam replied and went on to tell his host about the progress he was making on his restoration project. John, an equally enthralled car enthusiast, listened intently as Adam rattled off his plans for the Camaro in his garage. It wasn't until Ashley purposely cleared her throat that the men realized she was waiting for them in the kitchen doorway.

"Sorry to interrupt your muscle car jargon, but dinner's ready."

Moments later, the three of them were gathered around the table, enjoying the product of a great cook.

"This is excellent, Ashley. It certainly beats any frozen dinner I can whip up."

"I'm glad you like it, but save room for dessert."

A wide, childish grin spread across Adam's unshaven face, giving John a glimpse of the usual Carey. It didn't last long, however. Adam returned to his original state after dinner when John inquired about the journalist from Star Lake.

"I didn't think it would be this difficult."

John held back his smile of understanding and just nodded for his friend to continue.

"When we first met, it was like we'd known each other forever. Now, I realize that I *want* to know her forever. I want it to be like it was before she knew the truth."

"It will never be that way, Carey."

"I know, but I still want to be with her."

"Carey," Ashley spoke for the first time since they'd taken their coffee into the living room. "Maybe you should look at this from Katie's perspective. Women can't read minds. You can't expect her to forgive you without knowing the whole story. Believe it or not, she needs closure just as much as you do."

"What if she won't even talk to me?"

"Then you'll just have to let it go."

"And if I don't want to?"

"Only Katie can answer that question."

The blonde clearing the Sunday School table was captivating to look at. Lyndon leaned against the doorjamb unnoticed and watched Catherine sweep the glitter off the table with her hands. He honestly didn't know if she had started teaching again because she missed it or because she needed another diversion. Maybe it was a little of both.

If only he had a distraction other than her. His thoughts about her had changed. He used to think in a way that always revolved around their potential future together, whereas now he thought only of her happiness.

It had been difficult at first to put his feelings aside. Months ago, he would have just continued to push his way into her life, but not now. Concern was the one and only feeling that overwhelmed him, and he was going to be there to prove how much he cared.

"Lyndon!" Catherine exclaimed as she put a hand to her chest in surprise. "You scared me!"

"Now you know how these kids feel," he replied sarcastically. "So, how did it go? Your first week back?"

"Just fine. It's still just as challenging as before but also as rewarding. How was your Sunday School?"

"Good."

Lyndon went on to briefly sum up the lesson for her, while assisting in straightening the room. When they had finished, they walked together to the sanctuary.

"Do you have plans this afternoon?"

Lyndon looked surprised by her question and shook his head no.

"You should come over and watch a movie or something."

"Is Megan going to be there?" Lyndon knew that being alone at her house would tempt him to forsake his efforts at only being her friend.

"Why? Do you have a thing for my roommate?"

"Would it bother you if I did?"

Catherine opened her mouth to respond, but no sound came out.

"Speechless?" he teased her.

"No. I would never imagine that you were involved with her."

"Because she hates me?"

"Because she's not a believer. I trust that does mean something to you, doesn't it?"

"Of course. That's why I'm still looking. It's also why spending the afternoon in your living room alone isn't such a good idea."

Catherine nodded in understanding. "I'll see you tonight, then?"

"I'll be here."

Lyndon quickly made his way to his car. The weather was still very cold, and he didn't care to be out in it any longer than necessary.

"Thanks for meeting me here on such short notice," Catherine said as she slid into the booth Lyndon was already occupying. A cup of coffee resting on the table in front of him made him look absolutely relaxed, and for that she was more thankful than she could begin to say.

It was hard enough to call him and request his presence at the coffee shop late on the Sunday afternoon. Now, sitting there across from him, she wondered how she should go about asking him such an important question.

Lyndon studied her features for a clue as to why she had asked to meet with him. Her countenance offered nothing, though. Not that he cared. Any reason to see her was a good reason. "Do you want something to drink?"

"No, thanks. I'd rather get right down to business."

"Business? Is that why we're here?"

Catherine tried to give him a reprimanding look, but he wasn't fooled. Instead, he took a long sip of his coffee, never taking his eyes off her and then spoke.

"What's on your mind, Cat?"

"Work."

"What about it?"

"Do you think you could manage without me for a while?"

"You're not quitting, are you?" He tried to keep his voice from sounding desperate.

"No, I'm not. I just need a break."

"A break from writing, or just some time off from work?"

"Just some time."

"How much time are we talking here?"

"I'm not sure. Maybe a week."

"Are you asking for a paid vacation or a leave of absence?"

"It's up to you whether or not you want to pay me. I'm taking time off either way."

"You seem adamant. Are you asking or telling?"

"I wouldn't want to do anything without your approval. You are still my boss."

"Yes I am," Lyndon replied softly. "May I ask where you are going?"

"I'm not sure yet. Anywhere but here."

"Are you just trying to get away from me?"

"In a roundabout way, yes."

Lyndon looked stunned, then confused, so she went on to explain.

"I'm trying to clear my head of all things, not just you. I need to do some serious thinking."

"Then you're not going away to see him?"

"Is that what you think I'm doing?"

He just shrugged.

"I can't believe you think I would want to speak with that man, let alone take time off from work to visit him!"

"Calm down, Cat," Lyndon advised her. "Take it from me: feelings don't turn off like a light switch. It would only be normal if you still cared for him."

"I do care. That's why I'm going away, so I can have a good cry and get on with my life."

"Catherine," Lyndon began as he slowly leaned across the table and placed his hand over hers. "You don't need to go away to cry, or to do some serious thinking. And if you need to avoid me, then just tell me to get lost. I will."

Catherine looked down at his hand where it rested on her own. Never did she dream that they would be this close. He had been so domineering and persuasive in the beginning that she gladly accepted the idea of a relationship with anyone *but* him. Somewhere along the line, however, he had stopped pushing. The looks he gave her were no longer judgmental. In fact, on many occasions he had settled her shaky emotions with the confirmation in his gray eyes.

It was hard to believe that he was the same man she had once despised for his overbearing behavior. He still had it in him, when he sat at the head of the table in his no-nonsense suit and perfectly shaped dark hair. Even with her, he still played the role of her boss, except instead of setting deadlines and analyzing work, he watched her every move in order to provide her every need.

"When did you become so nice?" Catherine asked across the table. "You were so demanding and curt when we first met. You've changed so much over these months. It took place right under my nose and I didn't even realize. When did it happen?"

"When I realized that I was in love with you."

Chapter Ten

Catherine tried not to look surprised. This was, after all, something she already knew. Having him say it, however, was entirely different.

"And when did this happen?"

"It doesn't matter," he answered. "At least, not right now. I don't want to cloud your judgment anymore than it already is."

Catherine nodded in agreement. Her judgment, what was left of it, was not only clouded but on the brink of extinction. With the concern Lyndon was showing, it was easy to forget just how much she truly hurt inside. She didn't want vulnerability to drive her to him, and she was more vulnerable than ever.

"Well, church will be starting soon," Lyndon said as he stood and waited for Catherine to follow. "Just promise me you won't stay away forever."

A smile spread across her lips as she slid into her coat.

"I promise."

"It's good to see that you haven't forgotten how to work."

Catherine smiled up at her father and continued to divide slabs of hay between the cows. Her parents had been more than happy to have her come home for a week's visit. As usual, they didn't ask what had propelled her journey. Instead, they just welcomed her warmly.

"I was always afraid you'd forget farm life after you moved to the city," Evan commented as he worked along-side his older daughter.

"I would hardly call Star Lake a city, Dad."

"You know what I mean. Either way, I'm proud of you. It doesn't matter if you're writing columns or milking cows. You've never lost the ability to work hard."

Smiling to herself, Catherine hid his words deep in her heart. Like her, her father was not openly emotional, but they always seemed to have a special bond when they worked side-by-side in and around the barn.

"Leah should be getting off the bus soon. I'd better get back to the house."

"Thanks for your help, Katie."

"You're welcome."

Catherine's steps were light as she quickly made her way across the snow-covered lawn to the house. The once-familiar sound of the school bus stopped her at the door. With a bright smile on her face, she waited on the step for her little sister. When their eyes met, Catherine was once again amazed at how much the younger girl could change in a matter of weeks.

"Katie!" Leah exclaimed as she wrapped her arms around her sister. "How long are you here for?"

"Until the end of the week. Come in out of the cold! Tell me about your day."

"Forget my day! I want to hear about your life. Tell me everything," she said as they made their way into the house.

Catherine walked straight to the kitchen and began to make some hot chocolate for them both.

"I'd rather wait until Mom gets back from the store so I don't have to repeat myself."

Leah nodded, took her books out of her over-stuffed bag, and set them on the kitchen table.

"Fine. I have a ton of homework anyway."

"I'll sit here and watch in silent amusement," Catherine teased as she set the two mugs on the table and took a seat.

Leah looked skeptically at her steaming cup and then up at her sister.

"What? No whipped cream?"

"Beggars can't be choosers."

Leah nodded and took a sip of her hot chocolate just before she saw her mother coming through the back door, clad with grocery bags.

"Ah, Leah. I see you've met our dinner guest," Robin said calmly as she placed the bags on the kitchen counter.

"Am I the only one who didn't know she was coming?"

"No, but she's been here all day. You haven't."

"Oh well. Now that we're all here, let's hear everything, Katie."

"Shouldn't you be working on your homework?"

Catherine's attempt to change the subject was ignored as Leah just stared at her in anticipation.

"Do you really want to hear a story that has no ending and leaves more questions than offers answers?"

Leah only nodded her head, while Robin took a seat at the table with her daughters. Seeing no escape, Catherine began.

"It began the day I met Adam Carey."

Robin nodded but remained silent. As tempting as it was to interject, she knew it was best to let Catherine tell the whole story.

"He's the mechanic you've heard me talk about. I'm not saying that I believe in love at first sight, but the day I met him I felt like I already knew him. What's more, he felt it too. At first, it seemed wrong to deny Lyndon for a man I knew nothing about and was overly attracted to, but I kept my feelings to myself and played it off as being interested in Adam as a story. The few hours I spent with Adam seemed to surpass all the time I'd spent with Lyndon. As opposed to Lyndon's arrogance, Adam was shy and humble. I felt so comfortable with him that I forgot how little I knew about him."

"So, where's the catch?" Leah asked. "I would have thought you'd be halfway married to a man like that by now."

"I thought so, too."

"What happened?"

"My guess," Robin interrupted, "is that you found out who he was."

Both daughters stared at their mother in need of explanation.

"Adam Carey was there the day your brother died," Robin explained to her younger daughter while Catherine looked on in amazement. "He and Jesse were guiding the box together when the chain broke."

"You've known all this time and you ever said anything?" Catherine asked in an exasperated voice.

"I had an idea but wasn't positive. I wanted your interaction with Adam to be free of pre-supposed ideas."

"No offense, Mom, but that's a really lame excuse."

"Maybe, but you're a grown woman, Katie. I can't force my opinion on you."

"Just what, exactly, is your opinion?"

"Adam was in the wrong place, at the wrong time. He did everything he could to save your brother. I don't know much concerning his character, but he must be beyond reproach if he won your affection."

"I just don't know if I can forgive him for keeping this from me."

"It's not a choice. It's a command. I'm not saying you have to spend the rest of your life with him or even be his friend, but you do have to forgive him. You can't move on until you do."

Catherine remained silent as she calmly studied her hands folded in front of her. Asking her to forgive Adam was like requesting that she fly to the moon. The hurt from being lied to was almost as bad as being reminded, once again, that her brother was gone.

"There's just one more thing I'd like to know." Robin said, stealing Catherine away from her thoughts. "Where does this leave Lyndon?"

The name tugged at something deep inside Catherine. She had forgotten about the man who apparently loved her beyond words. The way he had stood by her, even when she fell for Adam, was admirable, to say the least. Whether or not it was admiration she felt for him, she wasn't sure. The only sure thing was the undeniable confusion pushing inwardly against her mind until she thought it would explode.

"Lyndon has been a friend beyond compare when I needed one most."

Catherine said the words almost to herself. The other two people at the table remained patiently quiet as they watched her sift through her thoughts. Several moments passed before she realized that they were waiting for her to speak.

"Why does life have to be so confusing?" she finally asked in the direction of her mother.

"As confusing as it can be at times, life's answers are usually right where we forget to look," Robin said as she pushed back from the table and walked toward the bags of groceries waiting on the counter. "In this case, I think it's right in front of you."

With that, she turned her attention to dinner preparations, recruiting Catherine to help. The subject was dropped, at least verbally.

Adam stared into the brilliant flames of the fireplace and slowly sipped his hot coffee. Although they darted here and there, his thoughts seemed to gravitate toward Katie and the pain he had put her through. It hurt to imagine her alone in the night, thinking of him only in association with lies and betrayal. Unfortunately, that was also how he thought of himself: a coward who's inability to forgive deprived him of any possible happiness. If time could be rewound and replayed, he would no doubt rewrite the script and alert Catherine to his identity the moment he realized it was pertinent.

Time, however, could not be rewound. Words could not be removed, replaced, or inserted. The reality of it all made Adam feel exhausted, but he couldn't bring himself to surrender to sleep. Taking another long sip of his coffee, he closed his eyes and tried to pray.

"Why is forgiving so hard? I've forgiven other people, so why can't I forgive myself?"

Maybe there's nothing to forgive because it wasn't your fault to begin with.

Adam wasn't sure where the voice came from, but it caught his wandering attention. For years, he'd heard others assure him that Jesse Scott's death was an accident and nothing more, but he'd never told himself that he wasn't at fault. Now, hearing the small, unexplained voice inside convinced him that he'd been wrong all along. There was no blame, no fault, no reason for guilt.

A sigh escaped his lips as he felt the weight lift off his shoulders. The pressure had been self-inflicted yet impossible to remove on his own. He had never realized that the pain and guilt could only be dealt with by divine intervention.

Slowly, he opened his eyes and set the now-cold coffee on the end table. Too tired to climb the stairs to bed, he stretched out on the couch instead and fell immediately into an exhausted sleep.

Catherine willed her hand to move the pen across the blank piece of paper, but it seemed content to remain motionless. Hours seemed to have passed since she'd taken a seat on the window bench in the room she used to share with her sister. She had been so intent on writing but hadn't penned a word yet.

Turning her attention from the page, she took a look around their homey room. The farmhouse had offered more than enough room for the family of five, but she and Leah had insisted on bunking together. Catherine smiled at all the memories that radiated from the walls.

There always seemed to be an abundance of clarity when she came home and spent time in this room. It was that clarity that she now craved more than anything. To be able to know which road to choose was a commodity she desperately longed for. That decisiveness seemed to remain just beyond her grasp.

Closing her eyes, she tried to go back to the beginning. She began with her fear. It had been so overwhelming to think of speaking to a mechanic face-to-face. That particular career field brought with it so many memories of her brother. Adam had squelched those fears from the moment their eyes met. As a result, her guard came down and she learned just how quickly one could become smitten.

Unfortunately, the joy of falling in love is equal to the pain of losing it. It hurt; the hurt was different than any she had ever felt before. Adam had been everything she wanted. His hard-working attitude mixed with his gentle regard, and blended to make the perfect potion, capable of sending her into a trance. But trances were dangerous and falsely secure. This was ever so true with Adam's spell.

If she were going to tell this whole story, she had to delve deeper into the plot. Catherine had indeed fallen for Adam, but what of the one who had introduced them? In the game, Lyndon had spent the majority of his time on the sidelines, waiting his turn on the playing field. The only time she'd ever seen him willingly lay down his pride was when her best interest was in mind.

Catherine smiled in relief at the truth she had just uncovered. She had set out to uncover a mystery about a man named Adam Carey and instead, although the mystery was solved, she had found that the real story, the real plot, the real discovery was right in front of her. A laugh escaped her as she shook her head in disbelief and picked up her dormant pen. This was indeed going to be a story unlike any other.

"Katie," Robin said as she looked up from the crinkled pages of notebook paper, "I had no idea you had this bottled up inside."

"Neither did I, Mom," Catherine admitted from across the kitchen table.

"This is the best piece you've ever done, but it's not how the words are written that has me shocked--it's the words themselves. You just wrote this?"

Catherine simply nodded her head in agreement. Never had words flown so feely onto a piece of paper. With each stroke of her pen, she felt another ounce of weight lift from her shoulders. The entire story took only a matter of minutes, although it was month's worth of revelations forming on the page. With the closing statement, she had rushed off to find her mother.

"I give it two thumbs up. I think your editor would be proud."

Mother and daughter shared a knowing smile.

"I don't even know what to do. This is the most decisive frame of mind I've been in for a long time. It's all so new to me."

"You've got excellent judgment, honey. I know you'll use it. For now, I'd like to enjoy the last day with my daughter before she goes away."

Catherine stood, walked over to her mother, and gave her an appreciative hug.

For once in her four years as a journalist, Catherine wished her desk faced the main office as Megan's did. Lyndon had been busy all day, too busy to welcome her back from her sabbatical. It was better that way. Or at least that's what she tried to tell herself. There was work to do on both parts, and he would undoubtedly begin to question things if she suddenly moved her desk to a different location.

Purposely, she had stayed at her parents' though the weekend, attending their church and leaving late enough to miss the evening service in Star Lake. She wasn't quite ready to speak with Lyndon. The drive back home had consisted of a very long and sometimes nonsensical conversation with the steering wheel. At one point, it represented Adam and her pain and hurt was poured out upon it. There were tears of relief from finally having the answers to so many questions.

Somewhere, Lyndon had become the recipient of her conversation. She had told him how his proud nature had softened around the edges. Or, was it she who had softened? Either way, he was the best friend she could have asked for and she was sure to tell him so. For now, she sat at her desk and tried to focus on work. There was some catching up to do.

"Have things changed?"

Catherine jumped at Lyndon's voice behind her and turned so suddenly that it hurt her neck.

"What?"

"You've been away for five days. Has anything changed?"

"Not that I can see. The coffee maker still works; everything else merely revolves around that."

Lyndon gave her that smile, and Catherine gripped the sides of her chair to keep from jumping up and wrapping her arms around his neck.

"I can't stay long. We're swamped from this weekend. That fire at the Bailey farm is big news."

"Sounds like a story I should be writing for you."

"You weren't here, so I had to ask Megan."

Catherine felt a tinge of jealously shoot through her. She had been gone for five days and already Lyndon had…

It was nonsense and she knew it. He loved her. Still, there was a creeping fear that something had changed while she was gone. Moving quickly or worrying about what to say or not to say wasn't going to help. Time was what they both needed. Her feelings, as new and exciting as they were, must be kept to herself. When the time was right, she would let him know that he had silently scaled the wall of her heart.

After the closing prayer, Adam gathered up his Bible with his well-worn hands and slowly made his way to the door. He felt ashamed for his lack of attention. The entire service he had tried to focus on what was being taught, but his mind was like a switchboard. His distraction wasn't from guilt, as it had been over the past four years; rather he was formulating a plan. God had given him a wonderful peace when he had finally chosen to forgive himself. Now, the only thing left to do was ask Catherine's forgiveness, not for his part in Jesse's accidental death, but for his deliberate secret keeping.

"You look good, Carey," John Warner commented as he stepped in front of Adam and firmly shook his hand.

"Thanks. I feel good."

John tipped his head to the side in quiet confusion.

"Care to explain?"

Adam laughed, adding fuel to John's already burning curiosity. It had been months since he'd seen Carey so at ease. The sight was refreshing, but still he wished to know the source.

"I've buried something that's been haunting me for far too long."

John had a good enough idea of what Adam was speaking of to nod his head in understanding. He and Ashley had been praying over the years that Carey would come to forgive himself. The change was obvious. John grinned widely and slapped Adam on the back.

"It's about time, Carey. It's about time."

Catherine awakened to a loud banging. She quickly rolled to her side and focused her sleepy eyes on the clock.

"Megan," she complained loudly, "it's three in the morning. What are you doing?"

She listened intently for an answer from her unruly roommate, but no answer came.

"Meg?"

The persistent banging continued and Catherine bolted upright in her bed realizing someone was at the door. Quickly sliding into her bathrobe, she walked two doors down the hall and peaked inside Megan's room. When she found it empty, it dawned on her just what was going on. Walking through the small house, Catherine thought back over all the times she had done this very thing.

After double-checking through the spy hole, she unlocked the solid door and opened it to find Megan, fist in the air, about to give another forceful knock. Catherine took in the sad sight. Megan stood unsteadily before her and gave a sheepish smile. Her bloodshot eyes matched perfectly with her slightly tousled hair and almost day-old make up.

"I forgot my keys," she slurred as she stumbled past and attempted to take off her coat.

"How did you get home?" Catherine asked as she assisted in removing Megan's coat and shoes.

"I, uh, don't know."

Catherine nodded and hoped she hadn't driven in this condition--again. Megan swayed back and forth slightly and closed her eyes to fend off the sudden feeling of nausea. Watching her closely, Catherine had a feeling things were about to go from bad to worse. Slowly, she began to lead her friend down the hallway. Megan had only taken a few steps when she dropped to her knees on the hardwood floor and threw up some of the liquor that had been eating away at her stomach. Catherine's own stomach churned at the sight, but she shook it off and reached to hold Megan's hair from her face.

"It's okay, Meg. You'll feel better," she reassured her as she gently rubbed her back with her free hand. "Do you think you can make it to your bedroom?"

With Megan's slight nod, Catherine helped her to her feet. The slow and sloppy walk to the bedroom seemed to take forever. Catherine pulled back the sheets just in time for Megan to collapse onto the bed. She shifted Megan's helpless body into what looked like a comfortable position and disappeared into the bathroom.

Returning moments later with a cold washcloth, she found her roommate staring expressionless at the ceiling with tears swimming in her eyes. Catherine brushed the hair from Megan's face and carefully placed the washcloth on her forehead.

"Close your eyes, Meg. Just go to sleep."

Megan attempted to object or complain but gave up and instantly drifted off to sleep. Catherine settled the covers over her. Staring down at her drunken state, she felt anger rise within her. At times such as this, she felt like more of a mother than a friend. This was not the first time she had played rehabilitation nurse, nor would it be the last. She was tired of dealing with Megan's failures. It was selfish, but she was so exhausted from the constant sacrificial mentality.

Lord, when is she ever going to believe? I've tried to live my life as a witness for You, but all she does is ridicule my faith. If I could just see some progress, I would be so encouraged.

Somewhere in her ranting, Catherine must have dozed off. She woke some hours later with a crick in her neck, leaning against the headboard. The morning sun was just beginning to stream through the bedroom window. Glancing down, she found Megan in the exact position in which she had placed her.

Glancing at the clock, she realized she could still get an hour's sleep before she had to get ready for church. Careful not to disrupt Megan's sleep, Catherine left the room and climbed into her own bed, thinking the sheets had never felt so good.

"You look tired."

"I am tired."

Lyndon took in Catherine's strained features. Her eyes were glassy and fringed with red. The stoop in her shoulders was as unlike her character as was her nodding off momentarily during the sermon.

"Are you sick?"

"No. I was up early this morning. Megan came home trashed again. I'm telling you, Lyndon, I don't know how she made it home without killing herself or anyone else. She drove home from whatever bar she'd been at. I woke up to her banging on the door at three this morning, claiming she had lost her keys. I checked this morning; they are still in her car's ignition. How can someone so disoriented drive a car? One of these times she's not going to make it home.

"If something ever happens to her, I'll never forgive myself. It's so hard to live with someone who toys with life and death almost every weekend. I know the truth, Lyndon, and that's what hurts the most. If she dies, she'll go to hell and all I can do is stand by and watch her throw her life away! I'm tired! I'm tired of waiting, tired of taking her ridicule, tired of being her hero. Sometimes, I wish I could just slap some sense into her. If only it were that easy, huh?"

With that, she let out a sigh of defeat, sprawled her hand over her face and blinked back angry tears. Lyndon's heart wrung with pain, but he didn't reach for her. Even in this, the most excusable scenario, he stayed true to his promise. Instead, he waited for her to look at him.

"Catherine, I know you're sick of being her babysitter, but you've got to keep loving her."

"That's easy for you to say. You didn't have to clean her puke off the floor this morning."

"Okay, I'm going to say something you're not going to want to hear. You may be the only person to ever reach Meg. You can't give up on her no matter how tired you are."

After a moment, Catherine held up her hands in surrender.

"I know, I know. I just want her to believe so badly. I just need a little patience." Seeing Lyndon's nod of approval she added, "Don't expect me to praise you for being right."

"I would never make you verify what we both already know," he answered smartly and followed Catherine out of the auditorium.

Chapter Eleven

The soggy February snow was still knee-deep as Adam trudged between the rows of engraved stones. His boots, as well as the lower half of his jeans, were soaked by the time he came across the grave he sought. Automatically, he reached up and removed his ball cap, nervously clutching it in front of him. The winter sun was a warm treat but blinding, and he squinted his blue eyes against it.

What now, Adam? he thought. *You traveled all afternoon to get here, and now you're speechless? No. It's just hard to get the words out. They've been mine for so long and now I have to share them. So, what do you say to a man who's no longer here? I blamed myself for so long. It's become rather normal to think of myself as a killer. Sure, it wasn't intentional, but it still happened. I took a man's life. There's no other way to look at it. I accepted it and was willing to live with the consequences. I had no idea just what the fallout would be. If I had known...*

But then Katie walked in that day and my life changed again. I didn't know Jesse Scott, other than talking to him briefly as we loaded the truck together, but I do know that part of me died that day. That same part of me came to life when I saw her. The void filled itself, and I couldn't understand why. I didn't know her. She didn't know me. But I felt different, alive, whole again.

And then I put the pieces together, and I still kept it from her. I was too ashamed to tell her what I'd done. I'd been holding it in for years, so it came naturally. She deserved to hear it from me and, like a coward, I stood back and let someone else tell her.

In her innocence, I found my forgiveness. She didn't hate me for killing her brother; she hated me for not telling her the truth. It's that truth that I've just found. What happened that day was in no way my fault. Holding on to it for four years was. It hurts to love her and not have her. But it hurts more to think of the time wasted in blame and guilt. I know now and I feel free because of it. I bet if Jesse were here, he'd tell me to let it go. And that's what I'm doing. It all ends right here, right now.

Adam replaced his hat and tipped his head slightly toward Jesse Scott's name. A relieved smile formed at his lips as he turned and began his trek back to the road. He gently ran a finger over the raised scar above his eye. *Thanks for the reminder. I won't ever forget.*

John Warner grabbed a soda from the small fridge in Adam's office and made his way into the work bay. Popping the top and taking a swig, he rolled up a chair and addressed his friend.

"So, how's business?"

"Good. The steady stream of snow keeps me busy with bodywork. There are plenty of accidents." Adam, standing beneath a lifted sedan, wiped another drop of brake fluid from his cheek. "Right now this brake line is killing me. The more I fix, the more I find wrong. I've been on this since lunch."

John nodded and took another sip of his soda. Every once in a while, he liked to stop in after work to chat with Adam. It was a time to relax and laugh.

"What's new?"

"Not too much. Life is just about the same--go to work, go home, go to church." Adam tightened down another union as he spoke.

"Don't make it sound so exciting."

"Well, that's what I do."

"I think we need to find something more for you to do."

"What do you suggest?"

John shrugged helplessly. "I'm not sure. You just seem so stressed, or distant, I'm not sure which."

"I'm just a little disappointed still. It seems ironic that I would fall in love this way. For years, I've struggled with being patient, waiting for God to give me just the right woman. Then she walks through those doors, and I think my life is about to change. She's beautiful, with long blonde hair, sea-green eyes, and a figure that makes a man check his sanity at the door. She is everything I've been waiting for, but I can't give her what she wants. I can't give her brother back."

"But that was an accident," John argued.

"I know that now, but I can't expect her to love the man who lied to her."

"I agree. How did she react when you told her?"

"I didn't."

"What?" John watched in disbelief as Adam walked to the rollaway toolbox and clanked his wrench into the drawer. "If you didn't tell her, then who did?"

"I'm a coward. I wouldn't tell her, so her boss did."

"So, you haven't talked to her since?"

"Nope." Adam wiped the remaining brake fluid on the front of his pants. "But I've been doing some thinking, and I think it's about time that I did."

"What are you going to say?"

"I have no idea."

Catherine stretched her arms over her head and soaked in the warmth from her electric blanket. Spring was coming on fast, and soon she wouldn't need the extra warmth. She smiled at the thought of sleeping with the window open and listening to the summer night sounds.

Work had been steady for the past weeks. Each night, she had come home exhausted. Tonight was no different. She had inhaled her dinner alone and was in bed by nine.

Sleep began to saturate her body, so she allowed herself to lazily think back over the day. She'd spent less than an hour in the office. Her day had consisted of braving the country roads, traveling to cover her story. The roads hadn't been dangerously covered with snow, but her car had been far from cooperative. The struggle with the steering wheel had drained her.

Sleep was just streaming in when a soft rapping sounded at her door. Thinking she'd imagined it, she rolled over and buried her head in the pillow, trying to regain her blissful slumber. When the sound came again, she peeled open her eyes.

"Cat, it's me."

"Come in," she answered automatically and tried to focus on Megan as she entered the dimly lit room.

"Oh, I'm sorry. I had no idea you'd be in bed this early. I'll just talk to you tomorrow." With that she turned to leave, but Catherine stopped her.

"It's okay, Meg. Come sit down." She patted the bed beside her. "What's up?"

Megan hesitated, deliberating whether to stay or go, then walked to the bed and sat on the edge. She stared down at the comforter for a few moments and then looked up at her best friend.

"For what it's worth, I just wanted to say thanks for always being there to help me out." When she saw the understanding in Catherine's eyes, her bottom lip began to quiver slightly. "I'm sorry that I'm such a burden to you."

"You don't need to apologize. Friends take care of each other, right?" Catherine tried to hide the emotions that flooded up inside her. Megan's gratitude was just what she needed to boost her spirits.

"Right. Well, that's all I needed to talk to you about. Goodnight, Cat."

"Goodnight."

Catherine waited until the door was once again shut and then let her head collapse back onto her pillow. Within seconds, she felt sleepy again. She closed her eyes and smiled, thinking of her conversation with Lyndon just weeks ago. Hadn't she been so ready to give up on Megan? It was as if God had sent another reminder to never give up.

Thanks, Lord. I needed that.

Catherine closed the blue folder and pushed back in her chair. Her assignment was finally complete, and it was going to be on the front page. It always gave her a sense of satisfaction when she was able to have one of her stories headlining the weekly newspaper. She smiled and greeted the copy editor as she handed her product over and was headed back in the direction of her desk when she saw Lyndon.

He was studying a layout with another employee, and Catherine knew better than to interrupt. He had been just as busy as the rest of them for the past few weeks. Telling herself to keep walking, she made her way past him and took a seat at her desk. Even as she absentmindedly sorted through her notes, she wished he would somehow find time to come talk to her.

The irony of it all was amusing. Once, in a conversation with her mother, Catherine had associated Lyndon with acting like a grade-schooler. Yet, here she was, behaving like a school girl herself. But wasn't she entitled to a little romanticism every once in a while?

No! I'm at work. This is no place for daydreaming. Besides, I'm not even sure of my feelings. It wouldn't be good to let them show.

An hour had passed when she once again pushed back in her chair and was startled by a yelp. She stood immediately and turned to find Lyndon's face wrinkled in excruciating pain. She did a quick survey of his body, trying to find where he'd been hit. His fists were clenched at his side, and he bit down on his lower lip as he exhaled through the corners of his mouth.

"Miss Scott," he gritted, "I think you just broke my toe."

Without waiting for a reply, he landed in her chair and closed his eyes against the throbbing. Sympathy clenched Catherine just before remorse set in.

"I'm so sorry, Lyndon," she tried.

His eyes remained sealed.

"Can I get you some ice or something?"

When he still didn't answer, she was at a loss.

"Lyndon!"

This time his eyes opened.

"When I was eleven, I pulled a stunt on our backyard swing set." He paused, and Catherine frowned at the random information. "Mix a swing, a metal slide, and a show-off and you get thirteen stitches. But that had nothing on what I'm feeling right now."

Catherine put on her best sympathetic look and suppressed the desire to laugh at his childish reaction.

"You think this is funny?"

Knowing she'd been caught, she made an earnest attempt to regain a sense of seriousness. The harder she tried, however, the more she smiled.

"You're laughing at me!" He tried to sound disgusted. "I'm wounded, and all you can do is laugh."

"I'm sorry. I can't help it." She even went as far as covering her mouth, but her giggling still broke through.

"That's it," he said as he painfully pulled himself to his feet. "You've just volunteered."

"What for?"

"To take me to the emergency room."

"Lyndon," she argued as he turned her toward the door. "Do you really think that's necessary?"

The stern look he gave was all the confirmation she needed. Grabbing her purse, she guided her hobbling hero to her car.

"You know, they're probably going to tell you to wait it out."

"Oh, I hope not. The least they could do is give me something for the pain." Lyndon, looking quite ridiculous sitting on the examination table, said as he watched Catherine inspect the room in boredom. "Or at least maybe my own personal nurse."

This comment caught her by surprise, but she continued to study the charts on the walls.

"You know, a really good-looking one who will wait on me hand and foot."

"Hmm, hand and foot, huh?" She opened one of the drawers and nosily rummaged through its contents.

"I mean, I'm going to need someone to help me during my recuperation."

"Recuperation?" Catherine asked, closing the drawer and turning to him. "Lyndon, you broke your toe. It's not open-heart surgery. It's not that big of a deal."

"That's because it didn't happen to you. Can't I get a little sympathy here?"

Catherine shook her head at his pouting features.

"You are something else, Lyndon Reinhardt," she said as she hopped up to take a seat beside him on the table.

"Like what, exactly?"

Catherine smiled and stared down at her dangling legs.

"I don't know. Trustworthy, I guess. Loyal. Predictable. Proud to a fault." She gave him a reprimanding look when he tried to correct her. "Honest." She paused at the realization of how much that meant to her. "Quite possibly the most amazing man I've ever known."

She nervously bit her lip as she waited for his rebuttal. Several seconds went by before she looked up at him, silently cursing him for his charming smile.

"And I thought you were going to be sarcastic."

"It's all true. You've never stopped being there for me. I don't think you could ever know how much that means to me."

"It's nothing, really. You're worth it."

He stared her down and wondered why she looked so uneasy. About the time he thought to ask, Catherine placed both of her hands on either side of his smooth face and kissed him soundly. The last few months of confusion and hurt, the collection of all her emotions, good and bad, were pressed against his lips in a desperate attempt to show him how she was feeling.

She'd been so blind, so infatuated with what she thought she wanted that she had written him off as a proud, intolerable sort of man. Now, the possibility of denying him only made her desire him more. She searched his face with her hands, testing him with her mouth, praying to find a reciprocation of love.

Extremely confused, Lyndon pulled back and gawked at her, gauging her sanity. A small, shy smile tugged at the corners of her mouth.

"Cat, I don't understand. What…? Why…?" he gave up when she leaned toward him again. This time he was ready. He captured every kiss she offered then returned it with emphasis.

The whole thing was puzzling. Wasn't she the one who had enforced the hands off policy? Hadn't she once scolded him for this very thing? With the tables turned, he understood the shock she must have felt that day in the office. Now, it was his turn to be the victim of a deliciously sweet attack. He was astonished, speechless. Not only were they kissing, which was something he thought would never happen again, but *she* was kissing *him*.

Catherine finally released her hold on him but kept her face close enough to feel his quick breaths on her lips. For several moments, neither one spoke. Catherine just watched in silent pleasure as he looked into her eyes, then at her lips, then her hair and back to her eyes again.

"You are full of surprises, Catherine Scott."

"And you," said the doctor from behind them, "do not have a broken toe."

Catherine quickly regained her composure, trying not to laugh at Lyndon's red face.

"So, um, what?" he tried, with everything he had, to come back to the present matter.

"We'll just give you something for the pain. Try to stay off your feet as much as possible, but other than that, time will make it feel better."

The doctor scribbled down the instructions and handed the script over to Catherine.

"Now make sure he takes care of that."

"I will," she promised as he left them. One look at her told Lyndon that she would.

Catherine did her best to keep both eyes on the road. Looking at her passenger would only distract her more. She knew Lyndon was looking at her, waiting for an explanation for her earlier actions.

"So," he prodded.

"So what?"

"Are you going to tell me what happened back there?"

"I am pretty sure I kissed you." She played along.

"Yes, I know that."

He waited for something else, but she offered nothing.

"Catherine?"

She finally looked over at him and graced him with a smile.

"I've been thinking," she began and turned her attention back to the road. "You and I are so," she paused to find the right words, "opinionated."

Lyndon tilted his head in confusion, wondering if he'd heard correctly. He had no idea where she was going with this.

"I never imagined it," she continued. "I never dreamed it would be someone like you. I was thinking more along the lines of the passive, easy-going type. And here I am, with you. You unsettled my world when you walked into that office. You took what I thought I knew about love and flipped it upside down. I am a very level-headed woman. You are a very goal-oriented man. And we, for some reason, fit. I'm just sorry it took me so long to realize it."

"Don't be," he cut in. "You taught me something through all of these months--patience. If something is important enough, then it's worth waiting for. I've been so used to having things my way for so long. Pushing the issue, as you know, got me nowhere. When I finally backed off and gave God the wheel, things began to change."

"How so?"

"I found myself wanting to love you, whether or not you loved me back. I just wanted to take care of you and be with you. I learned that love, real love, is selfless." For a moment he was silent. "What changed with you? What made you change your mind about me?"

Catherine thought back over the months but couldn't find any one thing that stood out in her mind. It had just been Lyndon's consistency, in nothing else but his devotion to her.

"Adam Carey."

Lyndon watched in horror as the words spilled out of her mouth. Of all the things that could make her love him, Adam's rejection had to be the lowest reason.

"Cat, I don't want to be a fallback plan. If you still like Carey..."

"No, no. He's here," she nodded her head in the direction of the office parking lot. Adam Carey stood beside his truck, hands tucked into his work jeans, looking anxious.

"What could he possibly want?" Catherine huffed as she pulled in beside Lyndon's car.

"I don't know, but I'm about to find out."

"Lyndon!" she grasped his arm. Her mouth opened, but she wasn't quite sure what to say. She wanted to tell him to calm down, that there was no reason to fight with Adam. She wanted them both to just get in their vehicles and leave. But inside, deep inside where she cared most for Lyndon, she wanted him to stand up for her. Looking at him now, she knew she trusted him in whatever he decided to do, however he handled the situation.

Lyndon watched as she slowly released his arm. He gave her hand a gentle squeeze of reassurance and opened the car door.

Chapter Twelve

"I need to talk to her, Lyndon. I have so much to explain, and I'm ready to explain it," Carey pleaded as Lyndon walked, very slowly, toward him. He waited until he stood in front of Carey to respond, not to add suspense, but because so much of his energy was spent in not wincing at the pain in his foot. Finally reaching Adam's truck, he leaned his back against it and shifted all of his weight onto his good foot. Ignoring the throbbing in his toe, he crossed his arms and took a long breath.

"I understand, but she," he said, pointing to the pretty girl in the junky car behind him, "has been through a lot. Maybe it would be best if you give her some time, or write her a note or something."

"Maybe that *something* could be me talking to her right now. I don't want to cause trouble. I've hurt her enough. Truth is she doesn't have to say a word to me. I just want five minutes of her time." Adam looked the part of a man in search of reconciliation. His eyes were soft, but his face had that 'man to man' look. "Five minutes, Lyndon. Just give me five minutes, and you can have the rest of her life."

Lyndon had to admit he had a good point. Catherine was in love with him. Sure, she hadn't said the exact words, but he knew he had her heart. With a little persuasion, she might even marry him one day. So, what could be so bad about letting Carey state his case?

"I take your silence as a 'yes'?" Adam asked.

"It's not up to me," Lyndon replied with his hands raised in front of him. "I'm just her boss."

With that he turned and made the slow trek back to Catherine's car, where she sat nervously playing with her key chain, refusing to look up even when he opened the door.

"He just wants to explain himself, Cat."

When she didn't reply, he lowered himself back into the passenger seat and turned his body to face her. "I'm not telling you that you have to do this; that's your choice to make. But, I do think you should hear him out."

Again, he was met with silence. Catherine wouldn't even look at him, so he had no way of knowing if she was even listening.

"Look, if you want, I'll go over there and beat him up. But I'd rather not 'cause my toe hurts real bad."

He knew this would get a response from her, and indeed she did turn to smile at him. It wasn't until she did that he saw the tears glistening in her eyes.

"Oh, honey. I'm so sorry," he said, even as the need to protect her intensified. "I can't even imagine how tough this must be for you."

"I want to, Lyndon," she spoke for the first time, her voice just above a whisper, "but I can't. I just don't think my heart can take seeing him again."

Lyndon needed no more. He was out of the car and giving Adam her answer in seconds. Naturally, the other man was disappointed, but knew there was nothing more to say. He turned and was gone moments later. Lyndon stood alone for some time, just to ensure that Carey wasn't coming back.

His mind went back to Catherine, and he felt his heart clench with hurt. It was obvious that her grief was still fresh. Much as he wanted to make a life with her, he knew it would only happen when she was ready. Only after she'd forgiven and let go of Adam Carey. He sighed at the thought. It had taken him years to find this woman, and it was going to be difficult to continue to stand back patiently as she worked this out. Just how long would she keep him at arm's length?

Without warning, he thought back a few hours to the emergency room. A boyish grin emerged. Well, maybe he wouldn't call it 'arm's length.'

"Lyndon…"

He didn't remember Catherine coming to him from the car, but she now stood by him and he prayed she wouldn't ask him to unveil the origin of his smile.

"How did he take it?" she asked, any sign of tears having disappeared from her face.

"It's not him I'm concerned about, Cat," he said as he let his arm rest across her shoulder and directed her toward her car. Only after he had her seated safely inside did he continue.

"Right now I want you to drive home and forget about this. Relax. Watch a movie, or take a bath, or something." Even as he spoke, Lyndon kicked himself for letting his thoughts run away to places they had no business being. He made himself focus on her eyes, though her lips were luring him in fast.

With a deep sigh, one which Catherine understood completely, he stood to full height and reached to shut her door. He felt his tie snag and looked in surprise to see her grasping it. She pulled gently, bringing him forward and sending his pulse into overload. With her other hand she touched his face, running her thumb over the whiskers that were threatening. Her own breath caught in emotion, causing Lyndon to abandon all hope of walking away. His eyes dropped to her lips, and he felt himself involuntarily move toward her.

Suddenly, her fingers were over his mouth. His eyes flew open and he stared in question at the woman whose face was just inches from his.

"I really am very sorry," she was saying.

The lost look on his face made her smile. Lyndon felt like an idiot. He was not following, and being this close to her was causing all his wires to cross.

"Sorry?" he finally managed, wondering if she was talking about their earlier kiss.

"For hurting your foot."

Understanding dawned on him, and he quickly backed away before she could draw him in again.

"You really are an evil woman," he said, trying to sound hurt. "Giving a man the wrong impression and all."

"And what impression would you prefer, Mr. Reinhardt?"

"The one you gave in the emergency room."

Catherine laughed out loud as he waved goodbye and hobbled his way to his car. She turned her own car toward home. It had been a big day and right now a bath was sounding pretty good.

Spring came on fast and found the newspaper staff behind schedule and working extra hours. Lyndon didn't mind the upbeat tempo. In fact, it reminded him of the office he had left to take this job. However, it was killing him to not see Catherine other than an occasional glance across the table or a knowing smile from behind her computer screen.

Most nights, she would peek inside his office just long enough to say goodbye, knowing he still had hours of work ahead.

Saturday mornings, he made his best attempt at sleeping in and then headed to the office around noon. Catherine's attempts to commandeer him on Sunday afternoons always fell short when he'd admit to being far too tired to give her the kind of company she deserved.

For a solid month, Lyndon felt as if he were swimming against the current. It wasn't until the beginning of April that the schedule began to clear. When the assignment folders were passed out in the Friday morning meeting, Catherine found a hand-written note tucked in hers.

> *Dinner tonight.*
> *My place.*
> *Six o'clock.*
> *Seating may be limited. Please arrive early.*

She hid her smile with a long swig from her water bottle. When she stole a glance at Lyndon, she found him listening intently to a report being given from the advertising department. Little did she know that he wasn't hearing a word. He was praying that he wouldn't set the kitchen on fire when a distraction like Catherine Scott walked through the door.

"You really should address the subject of intra-office dating."

Lyndon looked up from his paperwork at the blonde in the doorway.

"Has someone or something offended you, Miss Scott?"

"Oh, no, but if your employees are spending company time writing notes, they can't possibly be as productive as they should be." Catherine could see a smile forming on his face but continued in a serious tone. "Since you are the boss of such a company as this, I thought it imperative to bring this idle behavior to your attention."

"Thank you, Miss Scott, for bringing such a matter to light," he said as he stood and came around the front of the desk.

"I trust you will carry out the appropriate course of reprimand."

"Indeed, I will."

"Good," she said as she turned to leave.

"Catherine," he stopped her. "Aren't you curious to know what the repercussion will be?" His face was now outright playful, but Catherine held her serious exterior.

"Now, now, Mr. Reinhardt, that's between you and your employees. It's certainly none of my business."

"I'd be glad to make it your business."

This time her face reddened.

"Does this mean you're coming to dinner?"

"Absolutely."

With the weather turning warmer, Lyndon opted for a dinner on the back porch. He hadn't outdone himself with candles and roses, but he did intend to spend some long-overdue time with the woman he loved.

Although by no means an award-winning chef, he was capable of holding his own in the kitchen. He had chosen a simple but tasty pasta dish and was slicing some Italian bread when the doorbell rang.

"It's open," he called.

"Where are you?" Catherine asked, never having been in his house before.

"In here," he answered from around the corner.

She followed his voice to the kitchen.

"Something smells good," she said as she peeked through the oven door, her mouth watering at the sight of the bubbling concoction. "I half expected boxed macaroni and cheese."

"You're not disappointed, are you?"

"Not at all." She took in the two plates on the counter, each with its own perfectly sculpted salad, and hid her smile. His organization showed in everything. "Are you trying to impress me, Lyndon?"

"Not intentionally. I was just hoping for a quiet dinner with you. You being impressed would just be icing on the cake."

"There's cake?"

"No."

"Oh. Then, I guess I'm not impressed."

Lyndon let out a good laugh. For some reason, he had felt nervous about this. He had seen the change in Catherine's feelings toward him, but that had been weeks ago. He'd feared she'd changed her mind or that things might be awkward between them. They had shared an amazing moment at the hospital, but work had gotten the best of him, and he hadn't had an uninterrupted moment with her since. Now, he kicked himself for not somehow making the time.

"Are you all right?" Catherine was standing close to him now.

"I'm just glad you're here."

"You didn't think I'd show?"

"What I mean is that I'm glad we finally have some time together. I'm sorry it took so long."

She watched as he took the steaming dish out of the oven. She had missed him. Seeing him at work was not enough. With every day, she realized just how much she enjoyed his humor and honesty. And now, being here with him, seeing him in his element, she felt at home.

"It's not your fault. You can't control how many stories come in or how busy the paper gets."

"True." He began dishing out portions for them. "But it is still my fault. I need to get my priorities straight." He handed her a plate and then her salad. "And you are a priority."

Catherine felt her face warm from his affirmation. There was so much on her mind, so many feelings she wanted to share. But, suddenly she was blank. When he looked at her like this, he stole her thoughts. She looked down at the plates in her hands, trying to retreat back into her own safe state of mind. Seeing her food, she was reminded that she had not come here tonight to be lured into Lyndon's sentimental snare, as wonderful as it may be.

When she looked up, she found a teasing glint in his eyes and a suppressed smile on his ever so magnetic lips.

"Are you laughing at me?"

"No. I'm trying my best not to."

"If I weren't holding these plates, I'd slap you."

"I seriously doubt it."

"May I ask what you are laughing, or trying not to laugh, about?"

"What you're thinking about." He turned, grabbed his own food and started for the back porch, knowing she'd follow. He made sure she was seated and then made one more trip inside to fetch the remaining food. When he returned she was waiting, drowning in curiosity.

"You can't possibly claim to know my thoughts."

"Not at all. However, *watching* you think is very entertaining."

Catherine, feeling perfectly stuffed from the delicious meal, lowered herself into the living room's overstuffed chair. Lyndon had insisted she make herself at home while he made them some tea. So, she sat comfortably, taking in the room. From what she saw, he was no different than any other bachelor.

The walls were painted white with no paper or border. Pictures were scarce, as well as any decorations. The few commodities the room did have were neat, everything in its place.

Just like him, she thought.

Two sliding glass doors opened to a small balcony overlooking the street and the quiet neighborhood.

Perfect spot for a Christmas tree.

Catherine pictured the serenity of a Christmas morning, standing wrapped in her husband's arms by a magnificent tree, watching the snow build up on the ground below. And of course, the sun would peak through just enough to bounce off the diamond on her hand.

Where did that come from? She snapped back to the present, shaking her head. *I'm starting to sound like Leah.*

"What about Leah?"

Catherine all but jumped out of the chair. She hadn't heard Lyndon come back into the room.

"Oh, nothing. I'm just having a conversation with myself." She gladly took the mug he offered and brought it to her lips to stem any questions he might have.

"Be careful. It's…"

She almost dropped the tea in her lap, bringing a hand to cover her mouth. Her lip burned enough to bring tears to her eyes. Lyndon set down his own mug and was quickly at her side, taking her mug and then her hand.

"It's hot."

"I see that," she said as she blinked back the uninvited tears the stinging ensued. "I'll be all right. Just give me a second."

Lyndon didn't move. He just mindlessly stroked the back of her hand with his thumbs and stared at her in concern.

"Go ahead," she said, looking away.

"Go ahead?"

"Laugh at me."

"Why would I do that?"

She could see he didn't remember.

"That night at Roma's; you burned your tongue and I laughed at you. Now it's your turn."

He said nothing. She wondered if he'd forgotten the incident. He just focused on her hand.

"You do remember, don't you?"

He finally looked up.

"Marry me, Catherine."

Chapter Thirteen

Lyndon didn't know where the words had come from, but they were spoken and there was no taking them back. Even if he could, he wouldn't. His only regret was that he'd caught her off guard. She hadn't responded at all. She didn't smile, laugh, cry, slap him-- nothing. Her answer was a blank stare.

Good one. Now you've scared her off for sure.

Proposing was something he intended to only do once in his lifetime and he'd trashed it. Now, he wasn't sure whether to apologize or ask again. He leaned a little closer.

"Honey…"

"What did you say?"

"Honey."

"No. Before that."

Catherine honestly didn't know if she'd imagined or mistaken his words.

"I guess I just asked you to marry me."

He waited. There was sadness in her eyes. Or was it disappointment?

"Cat," he began, now kneeling directly in front her, "I know it's crazy. Well, I mean, marrying you isn't crazy, but this," he nodded to their clasped hands, "this is crazy. It's not fancy or in the slightest way romantic, and I know you deserve more than this. I don't have a ring and haven't talked to your dad. But," he slowly opened her hands and kissed each palm carefully, "I do know that I love you. That's all I have to offer. Please give me the chance to love you the rest of your life. Just say the word and we'll call it forever."

How on earth was this actually happening? Sure, Catherine was a girl and she'd thought about this moment many times over the years, but she had never pictured it like this. This was Lyndon, stern, obsessive Lyndon kneeling before her with his heart on his sleeve, all but begging to be the one she'd wake up to for the rest of her life. Was she really ready to make that kind of commitment?

"Lyndon, this is so fast. I'm not sure if I'm ready."

"I didn't say we had to get married tomorrow. We can wait until next year for all I care."

She still looked uncertain. The last thing he wanted was to rush her into an engagement. If he had to wait ten years just to avoid a moment of hurting her, then he'd do it.

"Do you love me, Cat?"

She hesitated, afraid of the power of her feelings for him. Love? Was that even the correct word? Seeing she was searching, Lyndon placed his hand to her lips.

"It's okay." He felt her sigh of relief. "I'm not demanding an answer. I want you to be sure. When you're ready, let me know. Until then, I won't bring it up again."

"Thank you."

"You're welcome." He pressed a kiss to her forehead and stood. "Now, what do you say we try this tea thing again?"

Megan switched hands and tried raking from the other side. The arrival of spring came with much yard work. The snowplows had deposited a spray of stones and sand on the edge of the lawn.

Raking the debris into piles was laborious, but she latched onto the distraction--Tim had dumped her. She had tried to focus all day, but again and again her mind kept going back to their conversation the morning before.

"I don't understand."

He turned from the sink to face her.

"Don't get me wrong, Meg. It's been fun. I'm just not looking for something serious right now." *He nonchalantly went back to shaving.*

"And when do you think you'll be ready for something serious?" *she asked sharply.*

He just shrugged.

"I can't believe this." *She grabbed her things and made for the door.*

She still didn't believe it. What a fool she'd been to think he was genuine! Just like every other man, he'd played his cards flawlessly. Short as it had been, it still was the longest relationship she'd had in a while. It was her fault for letting her guard down. She'd actually seen potential in him, but he was just like all the others; he'll entice you with some rich words, take what he wants, and then leave you with little more than a guilty conscience and a broken heart.

Sighing, she ceased her raking and glanced over to check on Catherine's progress. Her roommate stood, hands resting atop her motionless rake, so deep in thought she didn't hear Megan come up beside her.

"What's with you?"

"I'd say nothing, but you know me better."

"So?"

"Lyndon asked me to marry him last night."

Megan blinked in surprise. Surprise in that Catherine and Lyndon were that involved, but also that her best friend showed no sign of emotion about the subject.

"And you said no?"

"No, but I didn't say yes either."

"I feel kind of out of the loop. I didn't realize you guys were even dating."

"We're not."

"So, he just randomly asked you the most important question of your whole life?"

"Basically. I was totally shocked. I wanted to say yes, but I just don't feel a peace about it."

"Peace? I thought people get married because they're in love, not in peace."

Catherine shook her head. How could she explain something as important as knowing the will of God and feeling His peace?"

"Ah-ha," Megan nodded in understanding. "This is one of those 'God' things, isn't it?"

"I guess you could call it that."

"So, you don't know if something is right until you feel peace?"

Catherine nodded.

"What does it feel like?"

"I guess I never thought about it before. It's more than conscience, and it's definitely not an angel on one shoulder and a devil on the other. I would call it absolute certainty."

"Certainty that you're doing what is right?"

Try as she may, Catherine could not believe she was having this conversation. Since when was Megan interested in 'God' things, as she put it?'

"Certainty in everything. Knowing without a doubt that God is in control, and resting in His promise not to leave us."

"Well, if God's like other men, he'll be sure to leave me. Besides, promises are just a bunch of words. Nobody keeps them anyway."

"In humanity's six thousand years of existence, God has yet to break a promise."

Megan stared out into the street. Admittedly, God had a pretty good track record. It was one thing to promise to do the dishes, but to promise not to leave someone, that was admirable. From what she gathered, God was with her all the time. Why else would He promise not to leave?

"What other things does God promise to do?"

"Well, let me see…"

Catherine went on to list many things. Some Megan understood, and some were over her head. One, however, stood out: His promise of an eternal home in Heaven.

"Why would He have to promise that? It's a given for good people."

"Do you think you deserve Heaven, Meg. Because I don't think I deserve it."

"But, if anybody deserves it, you do. Look at you--you don't swear, you do good things for people, you don't mess around with men, you don't drink,"

"That means nothing. I do and don't do those things because they are a reflection of what I believe. They have nothing to do with getting to Heaven."

"If you can't get in, then I don't stand a chance."

"This is where the good part comes in. God promises Heaven to anyone, and I mean anyone, who believes that His Son, Jesus died to pay for our sin."

"And that's what you believe?"

"With all my heart."

"Why have you never told me all of this before?"

"You've never been this open before."

"I guess desperate times call for desperate measures. I think I'll go to church with you tomorrow. Not that I don't believe you, but it sounds too good to be true."

"No offense taken."

Both women smiled before Catherine suggested something cold to drink before they went back to work. They talked about many things throughout the rest of the day, but the subject never went very far from God and His promises.

Lyndon smiled at Catherine as she took a seat beside him in the pew. It wasn't like her to be late. It was then that he saw Megan also taking a seat. Although shocked, he still managed to lean over and whisper a good morning to her. Then he turned his attention to the honey-blonde next to him.

"Good morning, beautiful."

His tone coerced a smile from her.

"Hi," she managed.

He tried not to stare at her. On Sundays, she usually wore her hair down, which was luring enough, but today it was her eyes that caught his interest. They were very much alive and almost teasing.

"Lyndon, stop. You're making me nervous."

"Sorry," he said, not realizing he'd been staring at her. Before he turned his attention back to the front, he stole a quick glance at Megan. She seemed focused. Or was it dazed? Either way, she had her eyes fixed on the pulpit, which was more than he could do. He began to pray that what she heard today would change her life.

"I've got good news," Catherine told her mother later that afternoon. Much as she wanted to tell her family in person, the drive to and from home for such a short visit was just impractical. Instead, she waited until she had gained some time alone and then made her phone call.

"Two things, actually. First, Meg received Christ today."

"Oh, honey!" Robin exclaimed, her voice wobbly. "I know how long you've prayed for her. How did this come about?"

"She just broke up with her boyfriend and says it got her wondering if anything is permanent. Of course, she's still heart-broken, but, Mom, if you could see her face..." Catherine stopped, her own voice failing her. "I'm so happy for her."

"And I know you'll help her out. Don't forget that she'll need a lot of support and prayer. This is a new beginning for her."

A new beginning.

"Which brings me to my next subject," she took a deep breath. "Lyndon asked me to marry him."

"I know."

"What? How could you possibly--"

"He was here bright and early yesterday morning. And according to him, he didn't ask you to marry him; he told you to marry him. Untactful, uncouth, and ill-timed is what he called it. He's sorry that it came across that way, but not sorry he asked. He said you aren't ready, and that it was perfectly fine with him.

"Your dad gave him his blessing. Even though our first impression of him wasn't perfect, we know you love him. You'll be stable and provided for, and honestly, I can't imagine any man loving you more than he does."

"So, you think I should marry him?"

"Yes, but only when you're ready. Please, don't rush into this, Katie. After all, this is the rest of your life we're talking about."

"I hope I'm as happy as you and dad are."

"I know you will be. Just take your time."

Catherine hung up the phone with a sense of liberation. There really was no rush. This was the second biggest decision of her life and nobody was pushing her into it. She didn't understand why she wasn't ready; she loved being around Lyndon and wanted to be near him all the time. The personal-space violation would take some getting used to, but nothing about sharing a home and a bed with Lyndon frightened her. So, why was she holding back? What was she waiting for?

No answer.

That's okay. I've got time.

Opening her eyes, Catherine could see that Megan had been staring at her.

"What?" she asked across the picnic table outside the office. The beginning of May ushered in some gorgeous weather, which made up for the constant rain in the second half of April.

"Should I pray before I eat, too?"

"Well, Jesus thanked God for His food, and so we follow His example."

"From what I've been reading, Jesus was also single," Megan teased as she saw Lyndon coming to join them. "I don't see you following that example."

"Is Megan giving you a hard time?" Lyndon asked. The spring sun was bouncing off Catherine's hair, illuminating the sparks of green in her eyes. He stifled the urge to touch her, not wanting Megan to feel uncomfortable.

"Nothing I can't handle," Cat replied.

"That's what I'm afraid of."

"Don't worry, Lyndon. Sooner or later, she'll need you for something." Megan assured him.

"How optimistic. There's nothing like being second string," he tried to sound offended.

"Watch what you say, or I'll bench you," Catherine warned.

"Oh, brother," Megan rolled her eyes. "A boss and a coach. With you two together, there'll be no hope for the rest of us."

All three laughed and started in with their lunch, but not before Catherine and Lyndon shared a long look. Catching it, Megan shook her head.

It won't be long now.

With two no-hitters in the season, the Tupper Lake baseball team was ecstatic. It was a long way from the national record, but it was still a big deal for a small town. Catherine had quickly interviewed Mike, the pitcher responsible for the feat, just before the team's practice.

Basking in his fifteen minutes of fame, the eighteen-year-old was Mr. Popular. Every one of her questions was answered with cocky self-righteousness. When Catherine finished, the pitcher even had the nerve to wink at her and mouth 'call me.'

Now on her drive home, she shook her head at his audacity. The sad thing was, he'd probably have that mentality for the rest of his life. She turned on the radio to block out the smug adolescent.

Five miles later, she started to hear the hum. Then the steering wheel began to pull to the right. Driveways on Route 3 being scarce, she pulled to the side of the road and took a survey of her rust bucket. The right front tire wasn't flat, but it was obviously losing air--fast. She debated on what to do. The next town, she thought, was about ten miles, but that was just a guess. On a rural road like this, she really didn't want to take the chance of running the tire flat. Who knew who would stop to help her? She cringed at the thought.

As if it were summoned, a pick-up truck pulled up behind her debilitated car. Now, she wished she'd grabbed something from inside, a weapon of some sorts. It was then that she recognized the truck and its driver.

Adam slowly walked up to her. Catherine unconsciously crossed her arms in front of her, steeling herself for his words. It was plenty warm in the afternoon sun, but she could feel herself shiver.

"Hi."

"Hi," she answered, her voice unraveling a roll of caution tape around her.

He looked down at the tire and then at her.

"Need some help?"

Not waiting for an answer, he went to his truck, dug behind the driver's seat and emerged with a portable air compressor. Without permission, he opened her passenger door and plugged the device into the cigarette lighter. Two minutes later, the tire was its normal size.

"I'm going that way," he pointed in the direction of home. "I'll follow you to make sure it doesn't blow out on you."

He was so calm and collected. Catherine just stared. Of all the people to stop, this took coincidence to a whole new level.

"What are you doing here? I mean, where are you going?" For being a writer, she was having a hard time finding words.

"I'm on my way home," this time he wasn't going to hold back the truth, "from the Auto Warehouse in Malone." He could see her jaw tighten. "The same trip home I made the day your brother died." The hurt in her eyes stabbed him, but he went on.

"I was there, but you already know that. I may never get the chance to talk to you again, so I'm going to tell you what you don't know. Your brother was always so upbeat. I didn't really know him, but he made the tedious job of loading a little brighter. I could always count on a smile from beneath that hardhat. That day, I don't know what happened. We were just chatting, I can't remember what about.

"Then it was quiet, and everything went white. I couldn't think. It happened so fast. He was hurt bad and couldn't breathe. What was I supposed to do? I couldn't just wait and watch him die. But, the box fell. I wasn't strong enough. That image has haunted me for years.

"Look, Katie. You can blame me for not being honest with you, but please don't blame me for Jesse. I blamed myself enough for that."

Catherine surprised herself by keeping her tears in check. It had never occurred to her how hard it must have been for him. Guilt was a heavy burden to bear. She could only imagine how it must have worn on him.

"Do you hate me?" he asked.

"No. Yes, I was hurt by you, but I think we've both been hurt enough."

Adam smiled for the first time.

"You don't know what that means to me."

"I think probably as much as it means to me." She extended her hand. "Thank you, Adam."

He returned her handshake.

"For what?"

"For helping me to let go."

"You're very welcome. Now, allow me to escort you safely to the next town. From there, we can both get on with our lives. Sound good?"

Catherine nodded. They said their goodbyes and as promised, Adam followed her to the next town. When she finally arrived home, she turned off the ignition and just sat behind the wheel. There was liberation in her soul that she couldn't describe. She felt free, light. There had been such a grief weighing her down. The chords that had bound her heart were broken. The hurt that she'd unintentionally harbored was gone. It was the most beautiful sense of…

She smiled.

Peace.

Epilogue

Maybe she's won the lottery, Lyndon thought as he watched Catherine through his office window. He had noticed it earlier, when she was talking to Megan: an ear-to-ear smile. It had accompanied her to the morning meeting, and he had fumbled at least four sentences just from briefly looking at her.

Now, here it was again. This time, she was speaking to another employee at her desk. Her eyes were bright, and her occasional laughter carried into his office like a song. He had tried and failed many times already to get work done. Looking at the clock, he resigned himself to his present task, going as far as turning his chair to get her out of view.

Later, while locking up, his curiosity peaked again. Catherine always told him goodbye before she left, but today he hadn't seen her since the afternoon meeting.

Maybe she had plans with Megan, he thought as he punched the keypad, arming the building.

Switching hands with his briefcase, he was digging for his keys when he saw her. With her car now parked beside his, Catherine leaned casually against her door. Her arms were crossed, but her face was placid, giving up no emotion at all.

"I wondered where you'd gone," he admitted, walking toward her. She didn't respond, and now he wondered if something was wrong. "What's going on, Cat?" he asked cautiously.

"You may want to set down your briefcase."

Confused, he bent slowly and set it on the pavement, never taking his eyes from her. Standing again to full height, he waited for some kind of explanation. Still in office attire, Catherine's heels clicked as she closed the gap between them. Her hands locked behind his head and she pulled him down to her level, planting a firm kiss to his unsuspecting lips. Glad he'd taken a quick breath before her blitz, Lyndon was beginning to wonder when she was coming up for air. She was relentless, her arms concrete around him. Lyndon didn't dare reach for her. He wasn't sure if this resilience was anger or something entirely different.

"Lyndon," she managed and then drank a long breath. "I love you."

"You love me?" he stated more than asked.

"I love you." There was that grin again. "I want to marry you."

With a hand to her shoulders, he gently pushed her back. The grin momentarily vanished from her face when he reached inside his suit pocket. There was no little box to open, just a ring balanced gently between his fingers. This time, he was going to do this right. Her breath caught when his knee hit the ground.

"Catherine Scott, will you please, please marry me?"

"Lyndon, you haven't even asked me to date you!"

"You're right." He looked down at the diamond in his hand. "Catherine, will you be my girlfriend?"

"Yes."

"Good. Now, will you marry me?"

"Yes!" She barely got the syllable out before he was putting the ring on her finger, sealing the deal with a long kiss.

"It's beautiful," she admired, with her hands against his chest.

"It just compliments you." Lyndon leaned in for another kiss.

"How long have you been carrying this around?"

"Since the day after I asked you. I knew I had your family's blessing. What else was there to do than be prepared?"

"I'm sorry I made you wait."

Lyndon laughed and rested his forehead against hers.

"I don't mind in the least. You're worth that wait and the perfect reward for my pursuit."